The Case of the

SURLY SURROGATE

Safe Harbor Medical ® Mysteries

Book Two

Jacqueline Diamond

Published by K. Loren Wilson, Brea, California, USA

The Case of the Surly Surrogate, copyright © 2017 by Jackie Diamond Hyman

Cover art copyright © 2019 by Jackie Diamond Hyman

Safe Harbor Medical ® is a trademark registered with the U.S. Patent and Trademark Office by Jackie Diamond Hyman

For subsidiary rights, please contact the author at jdiamondfriends@yahoo.com or P.O. Box 1315, Brea, Calif. 92822.

This is the second book of the Safe Harbor Medical mystery series. It shares a setting and some supporting characters with the author's Safe Harbor Medical romance series. More information about the books and the author is available at www.jacquelinediamond.net.

ISBN-13: 9781936-505395

Praise for the Safe Harbor Medical Mysteries

The Case of the Questionable Quadruplet

"Love the mystery and medical setting interwoven to tell a great story. Lots of twists and turns and plenty of suspects to point fingers at each other. The end is unexpected and the reveal compelling. I will definitely read more by this author."
—Sandy Penny, SweetMysteryBooks.blogspot.com.

"This book keeps the reader on their toes as to who the culprit could possibly be from start to finish. The cast of characters is beautifully developed."
—Penelope Anne Bartotto, *Indtale*

The Case of the Surly Surrogate

"I liked this fantastic mystery. I never knew what was going to happen next and couldn't read fast enough to find out."
—Online Reviewer Jo-Anne B

"Attention cozy mystery readers: Jacqueline Diamond's second Safe Harbor Medical mystery only gets better! 5 Stars."
—Mary Castillo, bestselling author of *Lost in the Light*

The Case of the Desperate Doctor

"The mystery progresses at a swift speed and keeps you engaged with likable characters."
—Tracy Farnsworth, *Round Table Reviews*

Books by Jacqueline Diamond

Safe Harbor Medical ® Mysteries

THE CASE OF THE QUESTIONABLE QUADRUPLET
THE CASE OF THE SURLY SURROGATE
THE CASE OF THE DESPERATE DOCTOR
THE CASE OF THE LONG-LOST LOVER

Mysteries and Suspense

AND THE BRIDE VANISHES
DANGER MUSIC
ECHOES
THE EYES OF A STRANGER
HIS SECRET SON
TOUCH ME IN THE DARK

Safe Harbor Medical ® Romances

THE WOULD=BE MOMMY
HIS HIRED BABY
THE HOLIDAY TRIPLETS
OFFICER DADDY
FALLING FOR THE NANNY
THE SURGEON'S SURPRISE TWINS
THE DETECTIVE'S ACCIDENTAL BABY
THE BABY DILEMMA
THE M.D.'S SECRET DAUGHTER
THE BABY JACKPOT
HIS BABY DREAM

From the Author

Although I work alone on my character development, plotting and writing, the process of completing a novel also requires research, editing and feedback. I'm grateful for the input of friends, fellow authors and subject experts.

For his invaluable advice, I want to thank Orange County Sheriff's Investigator Gary Bale (retired). I'm also grateful to my beta readers, Deborah Golub R.N., Brooke Hamilton, Marcia Holman R.N. and Gail Ostheller, and to my critique group, Orange County Fictionaires. And a tip of the hat to D.P. Lyle, M.D., novelist and forensics expert, who answers complicated questions quickly and thoroughly.

Jacqueline Diamond
Brea, California
2017

Dedicated to the memory of my aunt,

Lenore Hyman Stillpass

CHAPTER ONE

Whoever killed Westlake Choate really wanted him dead. He was drugged, beaten, stabbed and left in a swamp.

The thirty-one-year-old photographer disappeared the morning after a Sunday dinner party at the home of his wealthy in-laws, the Bryerlys, which he did not attend. He had been hired for a wedding that kept him busy until midnight.

The next morning, as I later learned, Wes arose early and, without waking his wife, Cress, left their apartment above his studio. Since he didn't work on Mondays, his absence went unnoticed until afternoon, when he missed an appointment with his wife, the surrogate mother of their baby; and their obstetrician. That would be me, Eric Darcy, M.D.

Until the day when Wes was uncharacteristically late, I'd considered him only as the husband of a patient. I had no inkling how deeply my life was about to become entwined with his death.

For several years, I'd seen Westlake Choate around the town of Safe Harbor, California, behind the camera at weddings and other events, but hadn't had much awareness of him as a person until he and Cress began their infertility workup. Dark-haired with a trace of a beard, Wes was extraordinarily handsome and well aware of it. Toward his wife, he displayed a tenderness offset by occasionally insensitive remarks about her infertility.

It wasn't my job to like or approve of my patients, only to treat them as best I could. Moreover, experience—nearly ten years of it, since I graduated from Harvard Medical School—had demonstrated how often unsuspected qualities, positive or negative, might manifest in my presence.

Regardless of any mixed emotions in the marriage, Wes clearly adored his daughter-to-be. From the beginning of the surrogacy process, he had attended every visit, emailed me with questions and shared a couple of artfully lit photos of the bikini-clad surrogate, his fascination growing along with her belly. He planned, with her permission, to bring a video camera into the delivery room to capture the awe-inspiring moment when, in a painful gush, a baby enters the world.

I empathized with his eagerness for fatherhood. Although I'd originally intended to become a psychiatrist, partly to differentiate myself from my obstetrician father, I got hooked on the field during my medical training. Bringing a new life into the world, being the first person to touch that precious small person, was a thrill that never faded.

Just as I'd begun to dream of having children of my own, Lydia, my high-school sweetheart and the vibrant, volatile center of my life, had died in a still-unexplained fall while traveling. Now, thirty-six and widowed for two years, I felt powerful flashes of yearning to be a father.

Not yet. Not for a very long time.

My thoughts returned to the patients in my exam room, that Monday afternoon of Wes's disappearance. His wife, Cress, her long brown hair loose around her shoulders, checked her phone for messages as she paced. "I wish I knew where he is. He's not answering calls or texts."

"Great time for him to lose interest." On the exam table, her best friend and surrogate, Tanya Nichols, plucked at her skimpy gown. Buddies since childhood, the women often mirrored each other's facial expressions, gestures and manner of speech. Both wore their hair long and they dressed similarly in pink tops, white shorts and flip-flops. "I thought having a baby would be a big adventure. Well, I got part of it right. The 'big' part."

"The third trimester is always hard, especially in summer," I said. Despite the sea breezes, coastal Southern California gets hot in August. "I hope you have air conditioning."

"Not at my apartment," Tanya grumbled, tucking back a sweaty strand of blond hair. Most pregnant women radiate heat, regardless of the weather. "I'm still working, though. That's a good thing. Because of the A/C." An artist, she assisted at Boulevard Belles Photography—Wes's studio had inherited its syrupy name from a former owner—and advised clients on color coordination at Cress's bridal shop next door.

Cress and Wes had met when he popped into her store, Brides and Maids, to leave flyers. They'd told me that they'd progressed from joking about their rhyming names to sharing promotional ideas to falling in love. But when it came to having a baby, their luck ran out.

Unable to conceive, the couple had come to me for tests. Those revealed a combination of unexplained premature ovarian failure and a malformed uterus. Although Cress was otherwise healthy, their best option was sitting before us on the exam table.

Tanya, a former art student of my wife's, was an unusual surrogate, chosen by the parents outside of Safe Harbor Medical Center's surrogacy program. She hadn't previously given birth, which is normally a requirement, but agreed to carry their child without compensation beyond out-of-pocket expenses. They'd had a lawyer draw up a contract in accordance with California law.

Her participation, which included the use of her own eggs, had saved them a bundle. Luckily, she'd conceived on the first try.

"He left while I was sleeping. It's his day off, so I guess he went out to shoot pictures for fun and lost track of the time."

Cress drew a deep breath. "My husband's excited about this exhibit he has coming up next weekend. The wedding photography isn't his main thing, although he's terrific at it."

"Those shots he took of you are stunning, Tanya." I'd seen them proudly displayed on Wes's phone. "Are they in the exhibit?"

"No idea."

"He's keeping the whole thing under wraps," Cress said.

"You'd think it was at the Guggenheim instead of the Wine Arts Gallery," the surrogate added. "Unless this kid's in a hurry, I won't even be able to drink any of that wine."

"Why don't you go into labor in the middle of the reception?" teased her friend. "The exhibit would get a ton of press coverage."

"What, and steal all the glory? Wes would kill me."

"I'd kill him right back," Cress said stoutly. The mention of killing sent a shiver through me, although I'd never been superstitious.

I hadn't entirely recovered from the murder, the previous year, of an older client shortly after she consulted me about a puzzling set of circumstances. I'd operated on cadavers during my training and, as a doctor, witnessed a few deaths, but seeing my patient's helpless body stretched out beneath the glare of police lighting had left a permanent scar on my mind.

You can't save them all. Sometimes you can help them, though.

Being around these two close friends and the near-term baby dispelled my lingering shadows. "Let's get started, shall we?"

I don't like to rush patients, to the occasional frustration of my nurse. Still, we couldn't wait for a laggard husband who was probably stuck in traffic elsewhere in Orange County.

Identical nods sent me into action. Blood pressure: excellent. Weight gain: in the desirable range. Heartbeats of mother and baby: on target.

Tanya answered my questions about her well-being and the baby's movements, and we reviewed plans for the delivery at the hospital next door to my office building. I confirmed that the women and Wes had completed a childbirth class.

Attendance at such classes has dwindled in recent years, due to busy schedules and the ease of finding information—not all of it accurate—on the Internet. I recommend the advance training because my patients go into labor better informed and more confident.

"What a miracle." Cress gazed fondly at her friend's abdomen. "I can't wait to hold her."

We'd seen baby Georgette a couple of times on the ultrasound screen. But there's no substitute for the softness of a baby and the milky scent as she nestles against your shoulder.

"I can't wait, either. Georgie's started taking dancing lessons." Tanya rested a hand on her bulge. "Mostly in the middle of the night."

"I won't mind if she fusses." Cress beamed. "I'll take her downstairs to the shop so Wes can sleep." After a beat, she added, "Or he'll take her down to his studio so I can sleep."

"Like that's going to happen," Tanya grumbled.

"He will!"

"Yeah, if he's in the mood."

Early in the pregnancy, Tanya had treated both parents warmly. Recently, her attitude toward Wes had soured. It's not unusual for an uncomfortable mother-to-be to resent the father, especially if he isn't attentive in the foot-rubbing and tea-brewing department. In this case, Cress had taken charge of pampering and, it appeared, morale.

"I realize this is hard on you, Tan, but what you're doing is such a blessing," she said. "Georgie's everything to me. And there's only a few weeks left."

Tanya's expression mellowed. "It'll be fantastic to see her. And to put my real shoes on. How come you never told me my feet would puff up like cantaloupes, Eric?"

"Did I leave that out? Sorry." I don't mind when patients use my first name, since I often call them by theirs. Also, Tanya used to hang around our house with her older sister Shana, who was my wife's close friend.

Cress scowled at her phone. "Still nothing. I can't imagine what he's doing. Usually he's more considerate. Calling me. Bringing little gifts."

"Seriously—Wes?" Tanya's nose wrinkled.

"After five years, it's like we're still on our honeymoon."

"Or he has a guilty conscience," Tanya muttered.

"It isn't his fault women flirt with him!" her friend flared. "He only tolerates it because it's good for business. They're just tramps, anyway."

Red blotches dotted Tanya's cheekbones. Although they vanished quickly, micro-expressions reveal what's happening beneath the surface. It's a doctor's job, like a detective's, to pick up clues.

Those sexy photos of the scantily clad surrogate. Wes's cocky self-assurance. Tanya's change in attitude.

Had he seduced his wife's best friend during a photo session? While "seduced" may be an outdated term, the seething hormones and physical changes of pregnancy increase a woman's emotional vulnerability.

As far as I knew, Tanya didn't have a boyfriend to support her during this process. And a certain intimacy might well arise in an isolated studio.

I hadn't become part of this situation to facilitate predatory behavior. But perhaps I was reading too much into it. As a doctor, I tend to be protective of my patients.

I settled for hoping I was wrong.

"If you're concerned, you should report him missing," I told Cress. His absence did strike me as odd in light of his past reliability.

Her eyes narrowed as if I'd made an accusation. "He wouldn't run out on me."

What had inspired such defensiveness? "That wasn't the implication," I said. "If he suffered a medical emergency, it's important he be found quickly."

"Like a heart attack? At thirty-three?" Tanya scoffed.

"I was thinking in terms of a fall, depending on where he went to shoot pictures." Southern California's coastline and wilderness parks are dotted with cliffs and ravines.

Cress frowned. "Or his car died out in a canyon and there's no cell signal."

"Don't wait too long," I said. "In August, dehydration can lead to heat stroke. And young men tend to believe they're invulnerable."

"I've warned him to carry a water bottle," Cress said. "That doesn't mean he listens."

I could do nothing for him at the moment. "Let's review the signs of labor and when to go to the hospital."

Both women had questions, I provided answers, and we finished at around 5:30. Away they went, armed with print-outs handed them by my nurse. Cress was still checking her phone.

One patient remained, another surrogate accompanied by the intended mother. Almost eight months into her pregnancy, Maggie Mejia Majors had been diagnosed with a condition called placenta previa in which the organ providing oxygen and nutrients to the baby covers part or all of the birth canal. Unless it shifted by itself, a safe delivery would require a Cesarian section.

A cheerful young woman with a Hispanic heritage, Maggie was a familiar figure at Safe Harbor Medical Center, where she worked as executive assistant to the hospital's staff psychologist. Maggie had signed up for the surrogacy program because she loved being pregnant. She and her husband, a tow-truck driver, had two children and couldn't afford more.

I prescribed bed rest at home. The intended mother, Danielle Jeffers, promised to check on Maggie frequently.

"This baby means so much to us," Danielle told me as she helped the other woman to her feet.

"I'm thrilled to be a part of this." Moving gingerly as if to avoid jostling the baby inside her, the surrogate beamed at us both.

"So am I," I assured them.

Danielle's mother had been the older patient whose murder haunted me, and whose killer I'd helped to expose. But strongly as I wished she were here to enjoy this longed-for child, sometimes all we can do is move forward.

After they left, my nurse informed me we had an empty waiting room and no patients in labor. With a staff physician on duty at the hospital in case of unexpected admissions, I was free for the evening.

A blast of heat accompanied me to the parking garage, where I disconnected my electric car from its charging station. It rolled silently along the curving drive that serves the hospital and several medical buildings.

My sense of foreboding persisted. Tanya's changed attitude toward the father, Wes's absence and his wife's inability to reach him all hinted at trouble. Had I erred by not insisting the couple use the surrogacy program? Did Wes have instabilities that I'd missed? Legally, I'd done nothing wrong, but had I served my patients well?

You're their doctor, Eric, not their father confessor.

It isn't always easy to draw the line. I can be pulled into patients' private lives, as I had been after Danielle's mother was murdered. More commonly, I phone patients at home if I'm concerned about their symptoms worsening or if it occurs to me on further reflection that they might be withholding information, such as an inability to afford prescription medicine. While I don't receive enough free samples to supply everyone, I can share what I have to tide someone over until the next paycheck.

Stop obsessing about work. Although I'm never entirely off-duty, it's important to relax during free time. To refocus my thoughts, I concentrated on the people I was passing on Safe Harbor Boulevard.

From the Bear and Doll Boutique, a grandfatherly man emerged embracing a large stuffed lion and grinning. A young woman with her palm resting on her enlarged abdomen gazed in the window of the Baby Bump maternity shop. A little farther, a woman shepherded a boy and girl into a pizza parlor.

Children all over the place. None of them mine.

As I crested a rise and the gleaming harbor spread below, it hit me that with dedication, money—lots of that—and patience, I could commission a surrogate myself.

Longing welled up. To be a child's go-to guy, their father, their rock. To share a bond that endured throughout our lives.

I'd felt such closeness once, in a different way. As a high

school freshman mourning my mother's death from cancer, I'd connected with an intense girl who moved in the shadows of her father's suicide. We'd become each other's torches in the darkness and, despite ups and downs, set out on a course that had led to marriage and, I'd believed, forever.

Abruptly, two years ago, my light had gone out, for reasons I still didn't understand. Until I could move on, I had no business bringing a child into the world. Babies don't solve our problems, no matter how much we need them. They aren't put here to give their parents unconditional love, but to receive that from us.

Ahead, a green arrow pointed left. I turned toward my house, leaving behind a shimmer of longing. And, for a while, my unease about the missing husband.

But not for long.

CHAPTER TWO

For a solitary guy, I'd been lax about accumulating housemates, I reflected as I reached my small street. Deciding to share my Tudor Revival home with my father-in-law and sister-in-law hadn't exactly resulted in overcrowding—with four bedrooms and assorted nooks and dens, there was plenty of space—but far too much drama.

After my mother's death when I was thirteen, I'd lived here with my father, each of us respecting the other's distance. When Lydia and I married, Dad had invited us to live with him. We'd accepted gladly, and my wife, quiet as a rainbow, had carved out a private sphere.

Four years ago, Dad had died of a heart attack. Two years later, after I lost Lydia, I'd asked her affable stepfather, Morris Golden, to join me. Perpetually balanced on a financial brink, the caterer had been sleeping at his business and I'd been concerned for his health. He now occupied the downstairs bedroom.

Lydia's half-sister, Tory, a private investigator, hadn't waited to be asked. Following a burglary the previous year, she'd moved in, declaring it was for our protection.

I liked Tory, although her prickly emotions occasionally hit a flash point. You could have sold tickets for the fireworks during her break-up with my friend, Keith Sparks, a homicide detective, after she caught him cheating with a nurse. Specifically, having sex in an on-call room late one night when he was waiting to talk to a witness.

Not only had she moved out of their apartment and into my house, she'd quit her job at the police department and become a PI with a local agency. Eventually, she and Keith had achieved a shaky cease-fire. Very shaky, considering that he'd begun dating the nurse in question.

When I reached my driveway, I saw an aging red Honda Accord parked at the curb and wondered who it belonged to. No sign of the Golden Fine Foods truck. Morris must have been out delivering specialty dinners—choice of gluten-free, nut-free, vegetarian or vegan—to his subscribers. Still, this morning he'd left the fridge full of tasty leftovers from the Sunday night dinner he'd catered for the Bryerly family, Cress's parents. As one of the world's worst cooks, I was especially appreciative.

The garage door lifted to reveal Tory's green hybrid in the extra space, shielded from the heat. Usually she dropped it within walking distance of the curb, then raced inside to file a report on some supposedly disabled insurance fraudster she'd caught surfing, repairing his roof or—in one instance—training for the Ironman Triathlon.

I plugged in my car and, laptop bag in hand, was edging between the cars toward the inner door when it flew open. There stood the stocky figure of Keely Randolph, R.N., who moonlighted as my housekeeper on her doctor's two afternoons off. Much as I admired Keely's efficiency, it came bundled with the sharp tusks and temper of a walrus.

"I am not cleaning that room again," she declared.

I halted, since the only alternative was to bowl her over or die in the attempt. "Beg pardon?"

"Her office," she announced. I presumed that "her" referred to my sister-in-law.

My dream of a peaceful evening popped like a soap bubble. "May I come in?"

With a scowl, Keely allowed me into a small passageway. Straight ahead lay the kitchen, a broad expanse that opens to the great room. My mouth watered at the prospect of mining the fridge.

"That woman is out of control," the nurse/housekeeper declared.

"It's a pain when someone messes up a room you already cleaned," I said as politely as my hunger would allow. *Now go away.*

She plucked lint from her red-checked apron and tucked it into her pocket. "I don't know why she didn't do this earlier. No, she had to wait till I finished vacuuming and dusting. Then she shows up with a couple of guys and a bunch of boxes. Computer junk everywhere. Cords. Packing tape. Cardboard crumbles. Like they have no idea how to use a waste basket."

My brain was still catching up to the "couple of guys" bit. "I'll check it out," I promised. "No one expects you to re-do the room. You're free to leave if you've finished."

Keely's harrumph indicated her disappointment in my lack of outrage. "I have to fold the sheets and towels."

"Fine. Thanks." I deposited my gear on a table and headed through the great room and the three-story entry hall below a skylight. Beyond that, I heard male laughter and Tory's throaty chuckle from the front office that used to be my wife's art studio.

Bracing for the inevitable rush of emotions, I stepped into the glowing room where late afternoon sunshine diffused through the bay window. It had once illuminated striking wall pieces combining photos, paint and found objects, created by the animated woman who'd anchored my world.

Like a cuckoo left in someone else's nest, Tory Golden bore little resemblance to her petite, dark-haired sister save for a voice that eerily resembled Lydia's. Tall with frizzy chestnut hair, she leaned against her chipped desk, directing someone's skinny jeans-clad rear end.

"There's a power strip somewhere," she told the unidentified butt while acknowledging my arrival with a wave. "You're the computer genius, Parker."

"Plugging things in, not my field," came a tenor voice.

Parker. I knew that name. Not accustomed to staring at his ass, though. "They didn't teach that at Stanford?" I joked.

"They don't teach that anywhere," he shot back.

The third person in the room was my brother-in-law, Barry Golden, M.D., who spoke from the corner where he was straightening a printer stand. "You gotta earn your supper if you expect to eat with us, Park. Baked salmon, artichoke fondue and—what else did you say Dad cooked last night?"

"Epically unfair," replied the voice from beneath the desk. "You're making me work for my family's leftovers."

The denim-covered bottom, along with the red car out front, belonged to Barry's close friend and former college roommate. I'd run into Parker Bryerly often enough over the years to slot him into the younger brother category, along with Barry. Both were nice guys, pleasant to be around, without a lot of sharp edges.

Parker also happened to be Cress Choate's brother. I found it disturbing to run into him at my house right after seeing her at my office.

Last night, Morris had catered a dinner at their parents' home. Today, Parker's brother-in-law, Wes, had gone missing. The last time I'd encountered this many odd connections, one of my patients had been murdered.

You're getting paranoid. Cut it out.

"Hey, Eric," Barry said by way of greeting. A urologist four years my junior, he's shorter than his sister but has the same brownish hair and hazel eyes. Also, an easy grin that hopefully comforts his male fertility patients when he informs them of their lousy sperm counts.

"What's all this?" I indicated the computer gear.

"My laptop died." Tory shrugged. "Using my shiny new Visa card, I decided to go all-out for a desktop."

"Got it!" Backing out, Parker ducked his head to clear the desk. When he straightened, I glimpsed heavy dark eyebrows overpowering a diamond-shaped face, with wide cheekbones and a narrow chin.

"Thanks, Park," said my sister-in-law.

Grabbing a chair, he plopped in front of the computer and switched it on. "Let's boot up this baby and see what she can do."

Before he became too engrossed to tear himself away, I seized the chance to ask, "By the way, Parker, any idea where your brother-in-law's disappeared to?"

"Wes is gone?" he said. "That would be a bit of luck."

"Why?" I asked.

"Because he's a... what did I call him, Barry?"

"A pond-sucking dirtbag?"

"That's it."

Tory perked up. "Somebody need finding? Hire me. I have room in my schedule." While the agency where she's on staff, Fact Hunter Investigations, refers jobs to her, she earns more when she brings in clients.

"Please don't track him down." Parker's fingers blurred on the keys as the prompts whizzed past. "Do my sister a favor and leave him lost. He only married her because he thought she was rich."

A simplification at best. So I believed.

"The joke was on him," Parker continued. "My parents hang onto their money like a gorilla with a banana."

Did he understand his sister's marriage better than I did? He'd been observing it longer and at closer range. Or he might simply be biased against the flamboyant man who'd intruded into his family.

"Maybe he accidentally snapped a mafia hit man doing the deed and got offed," Parker added. "That'd be cool."

"Not really," Barry said.

Parker shrugged. "He wasn't at my folks' dinner last night, and I'm glad. All he does is talk about himself."

"Why wasn't he there?" I asked.

"Hired to shoot a wedding, he claimed. No telling where he really was, or with whom." Parker's nostrils flared in distaste. "We're better off without him. My sister certainly would be."

I wasn't inclined to joke about either murder or adultery. Neither, I gathered from the uncomfortable silence, was Tory or Barry.

Besides, we were wasting time that could be better spent eating. "You'll have to excuse me. I'm being paged," I said. "By my stomach."

"Done!" Parker hit Enter and various functions sorted themselves out on the screen. "Let's go."

I wasn't seeking company. Still, considering the dour nature of my musings, a little light conversation ought to be a relief. We all trooped out of the study.

Whoever designed this house must have loved to eat. In addition to a formal dining room, there's a greenhouse-style breakfast nook in the back and a butcher-block table in the open kitchen.

On the counter that separated the cooking area from the

great room, we arrayed containers of leftovers. While Tory commandeered the microwave, I piled a paper plate with chicken puffs, crab tartlets, stuffed mushrooms and cheese-filled pastries.

"Wow!" Nudging past me, Parker snatched half a dozen of the latter. "Spanakopita. Mom's favorite. And mine."

"Help yourself." En route to the table, I added fresh fruit. Chocolate-covered strawberries, to be precise. Very nutritious.

Tory took a chair, stretching her legs under the table and forcing the three of us to shift aside. "Spana... nakopita," she mispronounced. "That sounds Greek. I thought your mom was Italian."

"There's this phrase she likes: *una faccia una razza*. One face, one race." Parker spoke around a mouthful of food. "She thinks Italians and Greeks are practically the same. She and Dad never stop raving about a trip they took to Greece when I was a baby."

After fetching a bottle of Chablis from the wine cooler, Barry peered into a drawer. "There's a corkscrew around somewhere."

"I'll open it." Parker patted his pocket. "Hey. Where's my Swiss army knife, Barry?"

"I found it. The corkscrew, not your knife." As he uncorked the bottle, Barry explained to Tory and me, "I borrowed his knife to open some snacks. Didn't realize I'd be seeing him today, so I asked Dad to give it to him last night."

"Well, he didn't."

"I'm sure it'll turn up. If not, I'll buy you a new one."

The doorbell chimed. I'd half risen when Tory halted me with a gesture. "Don't bother. I hear the thumpa-thumpa of size twelve feet."

Whenever Keely was working, she took it on herself to answer the door. I once caught her holding the dryer

17

repairman at bay, demanding to know whether he had any communicable diseases. I advised her that medical histories are not required of service people.

A female voice rang out from the hall. "Aren't you Keely Randolph?" With a sinking sensation, I identified it as belonging to Narda Petrakis. That was Keith's new girlfriend, an emergency room nurse at Heights View Medical Center, located half a dozen miles inland. "Do you live here?"

"Housekeeper."

"But you're a nurse at Safe Harbor, right?" Narda persisted. "They didn't fire you, did they?"

"I beg your pardon?"

"I mean, because of your reputation."

A couple of years ago, Keely had accused the head of our fertility program of being an arrogant putz, which was true. She'd also once had a showdown with our former psychologist, who'd been widely and accurately regarded as a prescription-strength jackass.

Still, it surprised me that her notoriety had reached the staff of a neighboring city's hospital. And that Narda would be so flamingly rude.

"Second job keeps me too busy to go around bothering people," Keely snarled. Score one for her.

"Is Eric home?" That was Keith.

"They're eating. You know the way, detective."

Across the table, Tory stiffened at the prospect of seeing her ex-boyfriend and his latest squeeze. So much for our relaxed dinner-table conversation. It's a good thing doctors develop cast-iron digestive systems from eating on the run during our training.

Narda's voice grew louder. "This place is gorgeous! What stunning colors." I agreed with her about that. My wife had transformed the once-dark interior with hues of aqua, pearl and pink. "Who decorated it?"

"Lydia. Eric's late wife." Keith spoke softly, no doubt aware that we could hear them approach even though we couldn't yet see them.

"She had great taste." Narda's next comment puzzled me: "It's like being inside the Caves of Poseidon."

This house had never reminded me of a cave. A coral reef, rather, or an opal.

"What're the Caves of Poseidon?" Keith asked impatiently. He'd always disliked obscure references, which he considered pretentious.

"They're sea caves you reach by boat," Narda said. "My parents took me there when we visited my grandparents." Then she burst out: "This would be a perfect place to throw my birthday party!"

Say, what? "Like hell," I muttered.

Even my normally tolerant brother-in-law reacted with, "Chutzpah, anyone?"

In my household, we tended to toss in the occasional Yiddish term. Although I was raised garden-variety Christian, Lydia's family was Jewish. Not observant, although once in a while Tory lit Sabbath candles.

Rounding a corner, our visitors came into view. Narda, her dark eyes alight, greeted me with, "Whatever you're eating smells terrific, Eric."

"Thanks." Courtesy required that I add, "Won't you join us?"

"I'd love to!"

Tory uttered a low growl.

When Keith spotted my sister-in-law, he missed a step. Usually the six-foot-tall former football player radiated self-assurance. "Tory," he said. "Didn't expect to see you here."

"I live here."

"Your car wasn't out front." Regrouping, Keith made

introductions for Narda, although she'd met some of us before. Nods and hellos were exchanged.

At the counter, she zeroed in on the pastries. "I love spanakopita."

Two people in one day who could pronounce that word. Must be a record.

At the table, Narda dragged over a chair. "Eric," she said, ignoring everyone else, "hear me out. Friday's my thirtieth birthday. We were on our way to the party store to buy stuff for Keith's apartment, but this would be so much better! And"— waving a hand—"You've inspired me. Some drapes, some grapes, and we'll transform your house into a Greek temple."

"I'll consider it." *When we store frozen tissue samples in hell.* Scooting back, I went for my second course.

En route to the microwave, I nearly tripped over Keely, who'd knelt to stow towels in a drawer. "She'll turn the place topsy-turvy while I'm working on Friday," my housekeeper complained. "And leave a mess for me on Monday."

"I'll clean up," Narda promised.

"She won't," Keely opined, sticking to the third person. Judging by her snappishness, she hadn't forgiven the remark about her reputation.

Keith, who was piling his plate to a towering height, glared down at her. "This is none of your..."

"Stop there," I told him. "My housekeeper, my rules."

His jaw snapped shut.

"Pretty please," Narda begged me.

At the table, Tory's lowered brow reflected either displeasure or Neanderthal ancestry. Her brother cocked his head as if inquiring whether I had a death wish. There's nothing like family solidarity.

"Say yes," Keith commanded under his breath.

Surly Surrogate

Whatever I decided, I realized, shredded party decorations and spilled food would be the least of my problems. More likely, there'd be blood on the floor.

Most of it mine.

21

CHAPTER THREE

"A word before you answer." Setting aside his plate, Keith drew me into the laundry room and closed the door.

I could feel four pairs of eyes attempting to bore through the wall. That would be his girlfriend's, my housekeeper's, Tory's and Barry's. Our geeky friend Parker had shown zero interest in anything except food.

"What's Narda even doing here?" I asked.

My muscular friend stood a little too close, which I would have attributed to police tactics except that he's used that approach to intimidate me since junior high. Or tried to.

He's a big guy and tough as ever, despite a sprinkling of gray in his dark-blond hair. However, although I may be an inch shorter and lack his bulk, I'm not easily thrown off balance. Like police officers, obstetricians develop steady nerves to cope with difficult situations.

After a tense-jawed moment during which we both risked major dental expenses, he eased off. "She's been dying to tour this place," Keith said. "I didn't see any harm in popping in. It never occurred to me she'd pick it as a party house."

"It isn't."

He scowled. "Here's the thing, Eric. Narda's been angling to move into my apartment. She's hinting about bringing over clothes so she can change for the party. Once she reorganizes my closet, there'll be hell to pay evicting her."

"So either I wake up Saturday morning with a mess or you wake up with an unwanted roommate," I summarized.

"I'll owe you."

"What, exactly?"

"What do you want?" he asked.

A world of possibilities opened before me, none of them urgent. "Can I decide later?" Demanding a blank check was no more unfair than his proposing that I host a Greek orgy.

"Done."

When I broke the news to the others, Keely bared her teeth. "Bad idea."

"Are you always this crabby?" Narda asked her.

My brother-in-law peered under the table as if seeking cover. Barry's no coward, just smart enough not to tempt fate.

"Only when someone deserves it," Keely hissed.

Keith presented my housekeeper with a honeyed baklava dessert. "This should cheer you up."

Incredibly, it worked. After taking a bite, Keely sighed with satisfaction.

"Brilliant," Narda told her boyfriend. To Keely: "My apologies. I didn't mean to irritate you."

The housekeeper accepted her apology with lumpy grace. "Guess I woke up too early this morning. The coyotes were howling their damn heads off in the swamp." Her nostrils flared. "I mean, wetlands. Which stink, by the way."

Nature lovers cited the beauty of the salt marsh on Safe Harbor's eastern edge, a haven for wildlife, native plants and migrating birds. When I jogged past, I appreciated the swooping gulls and the bursts of color that dotted the gray-green sage scrub.

The problem was, dead plants and animals formed the base of the food chain. As a result, the place smelled like rotten eggs. And its western edge lay right behind the large house Keely shared with a group of fellow staffers.

"Well, I'm off," she said. Amid a flurry of goodbyes, Tory, her brother and his buddy Parker vanished toward her office.

While Keith and Narda ate, the nurse consulted party websites on her phone and kept up a running description of decorative items. Her excitement grew with every click.

Too bad Lydia wasn't here, I reflected. My wife used to love planning special events. One Fourth of July, she and a couple of friends—including Shana, the sister of surrogate Tanya—had created a tableau of white-wigged cut-outs of current political figures in goofy Colonial costumes. Their photos had gone viral.

Now that I was committed anyway, I figured Narda's party might be fun. And with only a few days for her to mess around, the damage ought to be limited.

I was almost looking forward to it.

*

On Tuesday morning, a couple of surgery cancellations allowed me to indulge in a long run. Although I enjoy my home gym, it's a pleasure to be outside in the early morning, inhaling the ocean breeze.

In such splendid weather, you might expect a crowd of joggers, but our neighborhood is tucked partway up bluffs overlooking the harbor and engineered with cul-de-sacs that discourage traffic. Too bad the tall houses tend to block the sight of the water, except for slivers of blue between them. And, of course, what you can see from your own view-blocking top floor.

As for the architecture, it's highly individual. My home's tall mullioned windows and dark half-timbered design contrasted with a white, New Orleans-style mansion I sped past, its wrought-iron railing gleaming from the balcony.

On the street behind and above mine, light reflected off a multi-level modern structure that seemed constructed primarily of glass. That was the Bryerly house, a familiar part of the neighborhood although I'd never been inside.

Parker and Cress's parents were the sort of wealthy socialites that everyone knows and nobody knows well. In an age of celebrities who parade their neuroses on camera, Noah and Bianca Bryerly maintained an invisible wall around their lives aside from appearances at charity and arts events.

Not that their origins were a secret. Anyone who regularly scanned the newspaper's business section, as I did, had run across their story.

A native of Texas raised by grandparents after his parents died in a fire, Noah had moved to San Francisco in the late Seventies. Before he turned thirty, he and a partner had founded and sold a major software company. He'd married his assistant, an Italian-American woman named Bianca, and retired young.

While vacationing in Southern California, the couple had fallen in love with Safe Harbor, bought a house and went on to produce a son and a daughter, Parker and Cress. Although both children had grown up and moved out, they remained in town.

My thoughts drifted to Cress's absent husband. There'd been nothing in the newspaper that morning about Wes's disappearance. Perhaps by now he'd returned home safely.

Her brother's antagonism toward Wes struck me as uncharacteristic. Parker might act competitive when video gaming with Barry, but in my observation he confined his biting remarks to politicians trying to control the Internet and companies careless about protecting customer data from hackers. I chalked up his dislike of Wes to a protective instinct toward his sister.

A meandering footpath led down from the street above. On it, I was surprised to spot a thin, shaky figure clumping along with what might be considered death-defying speed, considering that she was ninety-six years old and using a walker.

Lenore Bryerly, who'd been my father's patient and was now mine, lived in the glass house with Bianca and Noah, the grandson she'd raised. Now suffering from mild dementia, she sometimes took walks around the neighborhood with her caretaker, but I'd never before seen her out alone.

I broke stride until she caught up.

"Hi, sugar," Lenore greeted me breathlessly. "Aren't y'all just the nicest young man to wait for me." The Texas accent, pristine cloud of white hair and glossy red lipstick testified to her Southern upbringing.

"Glad to see you, Mrs. Bryerly."

"Dennis, sweetie, I'm glad I can still see *anyone*. Thank the Lord for cataract surgery." A smile creased her thin face. Hard to imagine it had ever been full and fresh like Cress's. She held her shoulders straight, though, refusing to concede the battle to weakened bones.

"Dennis was my father," I reminded her as we ambled forward. Since her street intersected mine a short distance farther, I planned to guide her home in a roundabout fashion. "I'm Eric."

"That's what I meant." She dismissed her mistake smoothly, accustomed to minimizing her dementia. "Y'all told me to get more exercise. And here I am."

"Indeed you are." I'd seen her a month earlier for a checkup. Like many women, she preferred to use her OB/GYN as her primary physician. "Any word about Wes Choate? I heard he was missing." When she didn't answer, I prompted, "Cress's husband."

26

"They found his car."

That didn't sound good. "Where?" I asked.

"Parking lot by the harbor. Last night." Marching forward, Lenore trained her gaze on the sidewalk ahead. "Darn. This walker's a rattle-trappy old thing. Wish I could find my cane."

I was more concerned than ever about the missing man. "Any sign of Wes?"

"Not a whisker."

Why had he left his car at the harbor? "Do you think he went sailing?" I ventured.

Her mouth trembled. "They never identified the other guy, you know."

Another trip into confusion-land. "What other guy, Mrs. Bryerly?"

"The one Saul went fishing with."

I searched for a connection. Despite Lenore's drifts of mental fog, I'd observed during her exam that an island of clarity occasionally broke through.

Ah, there it was. Her husband, Saul, had drowned seven or eight years ago in this very harbor. After his body washed ashore, a search had located his boat, which held fishing gear and an empty wine bottle. There'd been no indication of a companion, as far as I recalled.

"Why do you think there was another guy?" I asked.

"What other guy?"

"With Saul." In case I'd misunderstood, I added, "Or with Wes."

For a moment, Lenore didn't speak. Then she said, "My great-granddaughter's terribly unhappy."

Keep up, Eric. "You mean Cress?"

She nodded. "It's your fault."

"Mine?" I hadn't expected that.

"Y'all should show better sense," Lenore replied. "That girl,

27

Tanya. You put her right in the middle."

Was she referring to my accepting a surrogate outside the hospital's normal screening process? I hadn't realized she was aware of that. And what did she believe Tanya had landed in the middle of?

Too many questions. Since experience warned that I'd be lucky to get a straight answer to even one, I cut to the chase. "What does this have to do with Wes's disappearance?"

"Oh, look, here comes Georgie," Lenore said.

Around the corner trudged a heavy-set woman in a black dress with a long, brightly colored scarf wrapped around her neck. I recognized her as Agatha Kosma, Lenore's caretaker. About the same age and tank-like build as my housekeeper, she seemed to belong to an unacknowledged sisterhood of aging women who labor in the shadows of other people's lives.

Her name was not Georgie. Georgie was Lenore's long-dead daughter, mother of Noah and namesake of Cress's unborn baby. Tracking a dementia patient's declarations is a minute-by-minute challenge. My brain was getting a better workout than my muscles today, I reflected.

"There you are!" huffed the new arrival. As she drew closer, I caught the acrid scent of cigarettes. "Thank you for finding her, Dr. Darcy." Agatha, who'd accompanied Lenore on her office visit, spoke with a strong Mediterranean accent.

"It's important to keep her safe," I said. "May I suggest a personal transmitter?"

"Next they'll snap a leash on me," Lenore interjected. "Besides, they put GPS in my watch."

Agatha spread her hands. "We only think of you, Mrs. Bryerly. Your family does not wish to put you in a place. What do they call them? Where they lock you in."

"Prison," said her charge.

"A nursing home," Agatha corrected.

"They won't do that." Lenore spoke with conviction.

"Because they love you," I filled in.

"Because I know too much." She winked.

Agatha rolled her eyes and tossed her scarf, a splashy tropical print in pinks and greens. The gesture and the scarf provided a glimpse of a younger self who, I guessed, had been exotic and stylish.

After bidding the ladies a good morning, I set to exercising in earnest. As I ran, I sorted through what I knew thus far about the missing husband, including Lenore's comments.

I'd learned from Parker that Wes had skipped his in-laws' Sunday dinner party to shoot a wedding, and from Cress that her husband had left early on Monday, possibly to explore the artistic side of his photography. He'd failed to return for the afternoon appointment with his wife, the surrogate and me.

Now, according to Lenore, his car had turned up at the harbor, which might indicate he'd gone out in a boat. Reasonable enough, since one could capture dramatic shots from the water.

On the other hand...

Was Lenore right to suspect a connection between his disappearance and Saul's accident? Hard to imagine what it might be. As far as I knew, Wes hadn't met his wife until a couple of years after her great-grandfather died.

When I snapped out of my reverie, I'd covered more than a mile, reaching a dead-end street called Pelican Lane that runs along the wetlands. The breeze must have carried off the worst of the smell, because I scarcely noticed it.

Most of the houses that once dotted the flat street had been torn down, leaving an excellent view of the marsh. The remaining two-story stucco home was the property Keely shared with colleagues.

Behind the house, gulls swooped and mewed, hunting for

fish. A deep croaking call drew my attention to the east, where large, dark birds swirled around a fixed spot. Having taken a guided nature hike, I recognized several species: crows, ravens and a couple of large birds with brownish-black plumage and naked red heads.

Turkey vultures. What was it the guide had said about them? That unlike most birds, they used their sense of smell to locate their food.

A young woman had asked what food they preferred. The answer had been, the flesh of dead animals.

Coyotes howling early in the morning had awakened Keely. Now carrion birds were circling. Something lay dead in the swamp.

Please let me be wrong. I was not, however, inclined to trudge through the muck to investigate.

Swallowing my fears, I retrieved my phone and dialed the police.

CHAPTER FOUR

By the time a uniformed officer finished taking my statement, emergency vehicles crowded Pelican Lane. They included police cruisers, a crime scene unit and and an Orange County sheriff's vehicle, driven by a deputy I recognized from the coroner's office.

The coroner wouldn't have been summoned unless they'd found human remains. Was it Wes?

A cop's casual but chilling comment to a colleague drifted to me. "It's that software bigwig's son-in-law. Better call the P.I.O." The department's public information officer would run interference with the press.

My throat tightened. Unless there'd been an unlikely mix-up with the ID, Westlake Choate was dead. What had happened to him?

Cress had suggested her husband might have gone out to take pictures. The wetlands aren't normally dangerous. While he could have encountered a rattlesnake, their bites rarely kill adult humans. I doubted he'd run into a mountain lion in this flat terrain, and great white sharks kept to the ocean.

The main predator would be other people.

A black sedan slotted into a space at the curb and disgorged a broad-shouldered, blond man. Subconsciously, I'd been watching for Keith's red sports car, forgetting that he drives a police-issue sedan at work.

Homicide detectives don't investigate deaths from rattlesnake bites. Or mountain lions or sharks, either.

My friend stalked over. "No patients today, doc?" In his official capacity, he tends to be on the formal side. Well, "doc" is a shade more formal than "Eric."

I consulted my watch. "Actually, yes. Do you need anything more from me?"

After conferring with the policewoman who'd interviewed me, Keith said, "That's enough for now. Don't leave town."

The officer's eyebrows rose. Evidently, she didn't realize he was kidding. Or, I thought he was kidding.

"Wouldn't dream of it," I said. "Catch you later."

At home, I was relieved not to see Tory or Morris. That spared me having to relate this jolting turn of events.

As I showered, my thoughts churned. Whenever I break startling news to a patient, I don't expect her to grasp all the implications immediately. There are always more questions, and I had plenty.

Had Wes been murdered? If so, who had done it and why? How would his wife cope with being widowed as she awaited the imminent birth of their baby? How would their surrogate, Tanya, react?

As a doctor, I have no obligations to my patients beyond providing the best medical care and respecting their privacy. But these were hardly strangers. I'd known both Tanya and Cress's brother Parker casually for years. Moreover, I'd agreed to work with a surrogate who hadn't undergone the customary screening and whose mental state might be less than ideal.

Lenore's words echoed in my brain. "My great-granddaughter's unhappy. It's your fault." Absurd, of course, and spoken by a ninety-six-year-old with dementia. Yet after essentially stumbling across the body, I felt involved.

I considered phoning the young women to check on their well-being, until it struck me that the police might not yet have notified Cress. Best to hold off.

At my office, the news of a suspicious death in our town spread like a contagion. It started with a few murmurs at the nurses' station and by noon reached my partner, Isaiah Levin, who used to share the office with Dad. An easygoing fellow nearing seventy, he had a perpetual tan from the golf course.

"Isn't Mrs. Choate a patient?" Isaiah asked me in the hallway. "I heard her husband's body was found."

I nodded. "Their surrogate's due any day now."

"Damn shame. Well, can't be late for tee time." With a twist-of-the-hand wave worthy of Queen Elizabeth, he hurried off. Tuesdays and Thursdays were his afternoons to play.

When I ducked into the cafeteria to buy a sandwich, snatches of conversation rolled over me like the scent of frying onions.

"His poor wife! Aren't they expecting a baby?"

"Just saw him at a wedding Sunday night."

"Is he that chubby photographer or the hottie, the guy the bridesmaids drool over?"

Definitely the hottie.

In my private office, I checked *The Safe Harbor Journal's* website. No cause of death yet for photographer Westlake Choate, stated the abbreviated report, adding that his body had been spotted by a hiker. I was grateful the police hadn't named me.

Wes's fate remained in the back of my mind as I attended to patients that afternoon. Around six, I consulted the news again. The only update was, no surprise, that authorities were searching his apartment and car.

The car, I recalled, had been located by the harbor, a couple of miles from the wetlands. Not exactly convenient parking. That raised yet another question, one the police no doubt were already considering. How had he, or his body, been transported from there to the marsh?

My concerns, however, centered on my patients. How was Cress handling the loss of her husband? The strain must be affecting their surrogate as well.

Driving home, I noticed movement behind the large window of Boulevard Belles Photography. Although it might be the police searching the place, I rounded the next corner and pulled into the rear parking strip. No police cruiser or black sedan in view.

The back door stood open, and while I debated how to proceed, Cress hauled out a trash bag and slung it into a Dumpster.

In contrast to yesterday's shorts and top, she wore dark slacks and a blouse. Her brown hair hung limp and her eyes were rimmed with red.

I hurried out. "Cress? Are you all right?"

Her stare shaded into recognition. "Dr. Darcy. What're you doing here?"

"I saw someone in the studio and wanted to make sure you were okay." Heat rose from the pavement as I crossed. When she swayed, I grabbed her elbow.

"Sorry." She drew a shaky breath.

"Let's get you inside." I steered her into an air-conditioned hallway. "This has been a rough day."

Tears coursed down her cheeks. "It's horrible. The police went through everything. I'm glad they're trying to figure out who did this, but... Dr. Darcy, Wes can't be dead! I can't lose my husband!"

"I understand," I told her. "When my wife died, it felt like I'd dropped through a crack in the world."

"I forgot you'd been through this, too."

Hearing a noise, I peered down the hall but didn't see anyone. "You shouldn't be working. Let someone else handle things."

"There's straightening up to do since the police left, and Wes shot a couple of weddings last weekend. We have to process the pictures." The words tumbled out of her. "People are counting on us."

"You should be with your mother," I said gently.

"My mother?" Cress responded with a flash of irony. "She's not the supportive type."

While I wasn't acquainted with Bianca Bryerly, I've met enough women in my practice to know that motherhood doesn't necessarily come with a nurturing instinct. "Then call someone you trust."

"She did. Me." Tanya popped into view, her blond hair tousled.

"How are you feeling?" I asked the surrogate.

"I'm not the one who just lost my husband."

"You're the one who's eight-and-a-half months pregnant," I said.

Tanya's hand drifted to her bulge. "It's nice to have a doctor who makes house calls. And I'm fine."

"She's amazing." Cress leaned against the wall. *She* was clearly not fine.

"Let's sit down," I said. "Where's a good spot?"

"Through here." Tanya led the way.

Along the hall, I glanced into a large room equipped with cameras and lights, then an office and another room with a large computer screen, which Tanya explained was where clients selected their photo packages. The facility appeared too complex for Wes to have run alone, even with Tanya's part-time input.

"Is there a secretary?" I asked.

"A receptionist. She was here earlier," Tanya said. "Her mom owns the flower shop, Rose's Posies. We cooperate with client referrals."

"Very smart." I'd ordered bouquets there.

"She'll be back tomorrow."

"Good."

We arrived at a reception room lined with couches and blown-up photos of happy couples, young and old. These were the type you'd expect in a studio of this nature, unlike the close-up portraits along the far wall. Those subjects, mostly female, ranged in age from teens to seniors, their personalities unexpectedly revealed in the curve of a mouth or the vulnerable eyes. Wes's sensitivity impressed me.

"I like how he played with light and texture," I said. "His exhibit should be striking."

"The show!" Cress dropped onto a couch. "I forgot! It's scheduled to open on Sunday."

Sitting beside her, Tanya patted her shoulder. "I'll call the Wine Arts Gallery and cancel."

"No." Cress clenched her hands. "It's not fair to the owner, on such short notice. Or to my husband. Let's hold it as a memorial."

"There might be personal stuff that could be awkward," her friend countered.

What kind of personal stuff? I wondered.

"It should be exactly the way he intended it." From her pocket, Cress produced a wadded tissue. "I feel so helpless. Like I'm forgetting things."

She needed more grief counseling than I was qualified to provide. "Cress, do you have a minister?"

"No. Oh, my gosh!" She stared at me in dismay. "I hadn't

thought about the funeral. What am I supposed to do? I have no idea where to start."

That was the role family was supposed to play, helping you sort things out. Or a pastor or rabbi, if you had one. However, since she had neither a spiritual adviser nor a helpful family, the task fell to me.

I advised her to choose a mortuary to which the coroner could release Wes's body. The funeral director would guide her in planning the service and burial. That brought up another issue. "Has anyone notified his parents?"

Cress shook her head. "I don't know how to contact them. They weren't at our wedding or anything."

"Is he from around here?"

"From Oklahoma." Wes's parents, Cress explained, had divorced and each remarried several times, leading messy lives fueled by alcohol. There were a sprinkling of half-siblings, several of whom had tried to borrow money.

"One guy signed up for credit cards and a loan in his name. It was a mess clearing it up," she said. "Wes didn't want anything to do with that bunch."

"Be sure to give the police whatever info you have," I said. "They'll ask the locals in Oklahoma to make the notifications." There might be some pointed questions as well, I suspected, such as where each of the relatives had been on Monday.

From Keith, I've learned to take nothing for granted where murder is involved. Old resentments, family inheritances of which Cress was unaware, or mental imbalance might inspire a seemingly unfathomable crime.

To handle financial affairs, I recommended she engage an estate attorney. There was no life insurance to claim, Cress said; they hadn't thought it necessary until they had children.

"Now our baby will never know her father," she said. "Except through my memories."

"And his photos," I reminded her. Surely there were videos as well. I hoped that, in Wes's fascination with recording other people's lives, he hadn't neglected to document his own. "By the way, how did he get into the field?"

"He always loved taking pictures," Cress replied. "A class in high school got him started with photo editing."

Since discussing her husband seemed to calm her, I continued, "What brought him to Southern California?"

"He moved here about fifteen years ago, when he was eighteen," Cress said. "He started doing freelance work and hanging around celebrity events."

"He sold their pictures. I guess you'd call him a paparazzi," Tanya put in.

"Finally he saved enough for a down payment on this studio," Cress added. "I keep expecting him to walk in the door. The police and a coroner's deputy coming to my shop, I thought it must be a mistake. I guess everyone reacts that way, huh?"

"I did when my wife died." Since they both knew about Lydia's death, no details were necessary. "It felt like a bad dream."

"They interviewed both of us, separately," Tanya said. "They kept asking what happened at the dinner Sunday night. Which seems odd, since Wes wasn't there."

Had there been some special significance to the Bryerlys' dinner party? I was fairly sure Wes hadn't been deliberately excluded; he'd missed it due to a job. And since, according to Cress, he'd been alive the next morning, I doubted the police were double-checking alibis for that night.

"Oh, there's another weird thing." Cress paused.

"What's that?" I was curious about Keith's investigation, and since he'd already talked to these women, I didn't believe I was interfering.

"They asked how Wes and my brother got along. Honestly, they weren't close, but they didn't hate each other, either," Cress said. "Parker's always been protective of me."

I recalled Parker's description of his brother-in-law as a pond-sucking dirtbag. "Weren't close" was an understatement.

My phone rang. The readout showed Tory's name. Excusing myself, I moved into the hall.

"You on the way home?" my sister-in-law demanded.

"I will be soon."

"Hurry. Your presence is required."

"For what?"

"I'll tell you when you get here."

"Not good enough."

"Don't push. I've had a tough day."

"I'll bet it didn't start with discovering a..." Realizing I might be overheard, I cut short my protest. Besides, I was nearly ready to leave. "See you in ten minutes."

"That'll do." She clicked off.

Bossy woman. Tory used to treat Lydia and me with a measure of deference. Losing her sister and being betrayed by her boyfriend had toughened her.

In the front room, I returned to physician mode. "Cress, in case you feel like you can't cope, I'll send a prescription for a sedative to your pharmacy. I don't recommend taking it unless you really need it, though." Medication can interfere with a person's ability to work through emotions.

"I'd rather stay alert," she said. "But I'll keep it on hand."

One more thing: "Tanya, call if you experience any cramps or back pain or other symptoms. Don't wait until you're in full-blown labor. This is a lot of stress on both of you and it can affect your pregnancy."

"I'll watch out for her." Cress slipped an arm around her friend. "This baby is more precious than ever. It's all I have left of Wes."

"That's the truth," Tanya agreed.

They tipped their foreheads together. I left them there, comforting each other.

CHAPTER FIVE

As I drove into the garage, Tory flipped on her motor and gestured me to the passenger seat. Refusing to be rushed, I went inside to deposit my laptop bag, even though this required switching the alarm off and on again.

It's tricky, setting limits when my sister-in-law gets bossy. Since she lives in my house, I can't retreat into doctor-behind-the-clipboard detachment. As a result, establishing boundaries sometimes requires childish delay tactics.

That's my excuse, anyway.

"What's your hurry?" I asked when I joined her.

"Clients. Waiting." Her sedan swooped backwards into the heat, which was offset by a blast of air conditioning. When this car used to belong to Lydia, she used the A/C sparingly because it reduced the hybrid's fuel efficiency. Tory didn't give a damn.

"Since when do you take me to meet your clients?"

"Since they requested you." She whipped into the street in reverse. As with most trained police officers, she has excellent peripheral vision.

"Cut the guessing game. If this is a long drive, let me out." I'd had a stressful day, haunted by an image of Wes's corpse in the wetlands, even though the only thing I'd actually seen had been carrion birds.

"The Bryerlys live right around the corner."

Why would Cress's parents hire her? Then I recalled what Cress and Tanya had mentioned about their interviews. "I understand the police have been asking about Parker. Is he a suspect?"

"His parents think so." Tory tapped the brake at the intersection with their street, then shot uphill toward the glass house. "They didn't offer details."

If the Bryerlys' son needed clearing, of course they'd hire an investigator. "Why did they ask for me?"

Tory grimaced. "The old lady insisted. Mr. Bryerly said his grandmother has been babbling about her late husband and how you're the only person she trusts."

"I ran into her this morning." We swooped to the curb. "She showed up while I was jogging."

"Did she say anything of value?"

Good question. "In her opinion, there might have been another person in the boat with her husband when he drowned eight years ago. I got the impression she believed that was somehow connected to Wes's car being found at the harbor, but I don't see how."

"She's reputed to be senile." My sister-in-law shoved open her door. "Still, even a stopped clock is right twice a day."

Her five-foot-ten-inch frame unfolded in the fading sunlight. Instead of her usual jeans and T-shirt, Tory wore the gray slacks and black shell that constituted her new, self-imposed uniform. I gathered she chose it less because it went well with her tumble of reddish-brown hair than because she didn't have to think about the season or the occasion.

I exited cautiously. The road had been carved into a bluff, with no space for houses on the steep south side, where one could easily tumble down the brushy slope.

The site overlooked an impressive view of the harbor and ocean. You could also see my place below and to the right.

When I swung toward the Bryerly house, which had been built into the cliff on multiple levels, its walls refracted dazzling rays from the setting sun. Despite the abundance of glass, the interior lay as hidden as if shielded by stone.

"I was always curious about this place." Tory paced along the tiled walkway. "Barry used to hang out here with Parker during high school. He described it as 'way fancy.' Doesn't quite cut it, huh?" She pressed the bell, producing a musical passage from Puccini's *La Bohème*.

Noah Bryerly opened the etched-glass doors, his shock of white hair and the heavy eyebrows familiar from news articles and TV. Not that he sought publicity, but his younger self appeared in documentaries about the growth of the software industry and he occasionally dispensed mini-interviews to comment on new technology.

Sturdily built, he wore tailored trousers and a silk shirt. "Tory Golden? Dr. Darcy? I'm Noah." He thrust out his hand, shook firmly, and ushered us inside.

The high-ceilinged entryway provided cool relief from the heat. A few steps led down to a large living room with a polished wooden floor. Atop a rug with a fleur-de-lis motif, Italian-style furniture flanked a white fireplace.

Someone had exquisite taste. A safe bet would be the bone-thin woman joining us from the patio. Short black hair, a flowing wine-red dress and glittery sandals showed a dramatic flare. Unfortunately, the scent of her perfume failed to disguise the stench of cigarette smoke.

As Noah introduced us, Bianca Bryerly responded with a queenly nod. She cast an assessing gaze at me and skimmed Tory as if she were a minor player.

"Thank you for coming on such short notice." Noah

gestured us toward a delicate sofa.

I lowered myself cautiously, not trusting the couch legs. The furniture appeared designed more for show than for use. Seated beside me, Tory drew out her notepad.

Still on his feet, our host stared irritably toward the depths of the house. "Parker!"

With the slap of bare feet on wood, his son appeared, wearing a navy T-shirt that read, "Ask Me About My Superpowers." "Hey, Tory and Eric, thank God you're here. I can't believe the police are being such idiots."

"They've talked to you?" Tory asked.

"All of us," Noah said.

"Including your daughter," I noted.

Parker frowned. "I wish they wouldn't bother Cress. Honestly, I couldn't stand the creep, but my sister loved him."

Nothing about him rang false, nor did he come across as tense, the way I'd be if the police had me in their spotlight. From what I could see, he was exactly the same nerdy guy who'd crawled around under Tory's desk the previous evening. Hardly your typical murder suspect. However, I've been deceived before.

"Did you invite your daughter to join us?" Tory asked Noah.

Unless the Bryerlys had called Cress in the last few minutes, I was fairly certain they hadn't. The lines of communication didn't run strong in this family.

"Of course not. She's hysterical." Bianca spoke with a slight accent. That surprised me; I'd assumed she was simply Italian-American by heritage. "It's best her great-grandma doesn't see her in this state. Lenore's confused enough already."

She dismissed her daughter's reaction to widowhood as hysteria? Their family dynamics might not be my business, but they'd requested that I join this discussion. And that was what I intended to do.

"I met with Cress less than an hour ago." I leaned forward. Mercifully, the couch neither groaned nor trembled. "She's struggling on a lot of levels, and she could use your help. Planning the funeral, hiring an estate attorney, and especially emotional support."

"As far as I'm concerned, she's got it," Parker said.

"I don't see how our relationship with our daughter concerns her doctor," snapped Bianca, who remained standing.

Despite a flash of anger, I maintained a professional tone. "Her health may be at stake. Grief can have profound physical impacts. It can weaken the immune system, bring on exhaustion, and cause clinical depression."

"You're absolutely right, doctor." Noah shot his wife what I interpreted as a warning look. "We'll do everything we can for her."

"As a rule, it's best to keep all family members in the loop," Tory added. "On the other hand, avoid coordinating your testimony. You have to be honest with the police."

"That would be great if they actually listened." Parker sprawled across an armchair, more like a teenager than a man in his early thirties. "They insisted I go down to the station and talk to this uber cold fish, Detective Horner. Why not Keith? He knows me."

"That's exactly why not," Tory answered. "Parker, did the police focus on anything specific?"

The programmer nodded. "There was this text on my phone that I totally did not send."

"A text?" Tory prodded.

"Yeah, to Wes. Sunday night." Carefully, he recited, "'I know what you did. Meet me 6 a.m., the harbor lot. Don't tell Cress. You hurt her enough already.'" His nose wrinkled. "There were dumb abbreviations like 'enuf' and a frowning emoji. Seriously, a threat with an emoji?"

I wasn't fond of smiley faces myself. Or frowny faces, either.

"What did it mean, that you know what he did?" Tory asked.

"No clue. I didn't send it."

"Was the phone out of your possession Sunday night?"

"Man, you sound like the cops! I set it on the bathroom counter during dinner and forgot it." Parker gestured toward the interior hallway, presumably where the bathroom lay. "Anybody could have sent that. I left it unlocked. I mean, why wouldn't I?"

"You found the phone there later?"

"Well, yeah. Nobody stole it, if that's what you mean."

"Did Wes text back?" Tory asked.

"Yeah. Just 'OK.' " Parker wriggled in the chair. "I didn't read any of this until the next day. Whoever used my phone turned it off. Which, I might add, I never do unless it needs a reboot."

With the phone off, he wouldn't have heard notifications or spotted either message in time to text Wes and cancel the meeting.

What damning information had Wes believed Parker knew, and why would it have hurt Cress? Whatever it was, it had motivated Wes to rise early on Monday and drive to the harbor. Yet when someone other than Parker met him at the lot, why hadn't he been suspicious?

Maybe he had. Just not suspicious enough to run for his life.

"When you saw the text, did you report it to the police?" Tory's question drew me back to the present.

"No," Parker said. "All kinds of crap shows up on my cell."

"How did they find out, then?"

"It was on Wes's phone, too."

The killing had not been a robbery, I registered. Someone had deliberately arranged the meeting.

"The police took your phone as evidence?" my sister-in-law continued.

"Yeah. I had to get a replacement. What a pain."

"What else did they take?" Tory asked.

"My hard drive and other stuff from my apartment." Parker's lip curled in disdain. "I bet they're trying to get a warrant for the computers at my office. Can you imagine? My company has proprietary programming."

"Not to mention searching our house." His father began to pace around the circle where Tory, Parker and I sat. The loss of control obviously disturbed him.

"It was ugly. I feel violated." Mrs. Bryerly patted her pocket. Desperate for a cigarette?

"Can you think of anyone present Sunday night who might have wanted to kill your son-in-law?" Tory asked.

"We assume someone sneaked in," Noah answered. "We don't lock the doors when we're home and awake."

"Good thing I have an alibi for Monday morning," Parker said.

There was a rustling noise as everyone shifted to look at him. This appeared to be news to his parents.

"With witnesses?" Tory asked.

"On both coasts." He grinned.

She didn't. "What's the alibi?"

Normally, Parker said, he arrived at work around ten or eleven, then stayed late. On Monday, however, his presence had been required for a staff videoconference with an East Coast company at seven a.m. to accommodate the three-hour time difference.

Tory scribbled in her notebook. "The text said to meet at six a.m., and you didn't have to be at work until seven."

"I got there a few minutes early," Parker said. "And I mean, if I was out in that swamp with Wes, I'd have had to shower and change, right?"

Tory tapped her pen against the pad. "Who was aware of

your schedule that day, aside from coworkers?"

"Nobody, I guess." Parker dragged his fingers through his springy hair. "Wow. The killer figured I'd be home with no alibi, huh? It's, like, a frame job."

I'd drawn the same conclusion. Someone had arranged this carefully.

"I need a list of everyone present at the dinner," Tory said.

"Only family." Noah gripped the back of his son's chair. "My wife and me, our children and my grandmother."

"And that friend of Cress's, the pregnant one," Bianca said.

The word "icy" didn't begin to describe this woman. She must have encountered her daughter's best friend frequently over the years and now the surrogate was carrying her grandchild. But to Bianca, Tanya amounted to no more than "that friend of Cress's."

"What about staff?" Tory inquired.

Having eaten the leftovers, I could answer that. "Morris, for one."

"Dad gets around," Tory observed dryly.

Parker snorted. "Your dad wouldn't hurt a fly unless it tried to land on his salmon mousse."

Noah's forehead creased. "I didn't make the connection. Your father was our caterer."

"If that's a problem, I can recommend another detective at Fact Hunter," Tory said.

"No! We're sticking with you." Parker didn't wait for his parents' confirmation. "Agatha helped serve. She lives here."

"Anyone else?" Tory put in.

There wasn't.

"Any house keys floating around?"

"No. We're careful about that," Bianca said. "As my husband mentioned, someone could have sneaked in, though." Unable to restrain her addiction any longer, she drew out a cigarette and lit it.

A moment later, Agatha padded into the room in tasseled slippers. After sliding an ashtray onto an end table near Bianca, she retreated. Had she been listening in, or caught the scent of smoke from another room?

"I'm in the clear, right, Tory?" Parker pressed. "I mean, because of that teleconference."

"There's wiggle room with the timing," she said.

"Oh, come on!"

"It sounds as if this was a well-organized murder," my sister-in-law responded. "The killer planned it, from getting hold of your phone to writing a text that would lure Wes to the harbor without alerting your sister. And at an hour when you'd normally be home alone."

"Yeah. He messed up about my schedule," Parker said with satisfaction.

"Or the police may believe you arranged it that way to have an alibi," Tory said.

Parker smacked his hands on the chair arms. "I had nothing to do with this!"

"Could someone have cloned your phone so it appeared the text came from you?" Tory asked.

Parker's mouth twisted. "Yeah, on Wes's phone. But the text also showed up on my phone as having been sent."

"That couldn't be faked?"

"I don't see how. But there's always new stuff around." He looked to his father. "Well, Dad? You're the tech guru."

Noah spread his hands. "Let me think about it."

"Speaking of police, we're counting on you to tell us what they find, since you're an ex-cop." Bianca drew on her cigarette.

"They won't discuss their investigation. Revealing details to me could compromise their case," Tory said. "However, I understand their process and I'll retrace their steps, interview witnesses and pry out evidence they might miss."

"Yeah, like all of it," Parker muttered.

"If they do charge you, I can assist with your defense."

"Charge me?" He shot out of his seat. "You're kidding!"

Either he was the most arrogant killer around or he had nothing to do with Wes's murder. I'd have bet on innocence.

"Do you have an attorney?" Tory asked. "You should."

"I put in a call," Noah said.

"Dad! Really?"

"It seemed sensible."

"Mind if I ask who?" Tory inquired.

"Joseph Noriega. I've seen his name in the newspaper. Seems successful." What a contrast between father and son, I thought. Noah was thinking ahead, while Parker kept acting gobsmacked.

He recovered fast, though. "My own lawyer," he said. "Cool."

"Any other suggestions?" Noah asked Tory.

"Keep your lawyer and me informed about any information you turn up," she said. "Also, avoid the press."

Bianca stubbed out her cigarette butt in the ashtray. "Those jackals. They're always hounding celebrities at the fashion shows in New York and Milan. I can deal with them."

"It's best not to speak to them at all," Tory cautioned. "Especially you, Parker. You have an instinct to trust people. They'll twist whatever you say."

"This is awful," he said. "But not as bad as what Cress is going through. It's okay if I visit her, right?"

"Frankly, I'd advise you not to be alone with the victim's wife while you may be under suspicion," Tory said.

Impressive, that she had an immediate, knowledgeable answer to every question. Not that I'd expected any less.

"She's my sister!"

"If you can't stay away, have someone else present."

Extracting papers from her purse, Tory handed them to Noah. "I brought a copy of our standard contract."

He leafed through it. "This appears to be in order. Let me write you a check."

"I'll stay in touch and send regular reports."

"Excellent." Noah glanced at me. "Thanks for joining us, Dr. Darcy. My grandmother nearly had a fit when we hesitated to include you. I'll admit, I'm surprised that an obstetrician moonlights as a PI."

"I don't," I said. "But I'm concerned about your daughter and her surrogate. As long as it doesn't violate patient confidentiality, I'll assist any way I can."

"Good enough."

"And you're smart." Parker cast me a crooked grin. "Smart enough to find Wes's body before the police did. Yeah, I figured out it was you. Now that you and Tory are on our team, I feel better."

"Let's take it one step at a time." Tory had never been the optimistic type.

I tended to side with Parker. While his dislike of his brother-in-law and that text sent from his phone struck me as suspicious, they didn't prove guilt.

We'd shaken hands and were halfway to the door before he brought up the one thing I really didn't want to hear.

"I just wish I knew what happened to my knife," Parker said.

CHAPTER SIX

Everyone froze. I reminded myself to breathe.

"No big deal," Parker said. "Barry promised to buy me a new one."

Could anyone be that clueless?

"Unless it turns out to be the murder weapon," Tory muttered.

Parker's brown eyes went so wide, he popped a contact lens. It landed in the palm of his hand. "Murder weapon?" He stared at the lens as if an alien had dropped it there.

"Speaking of that, what *did* kill our son-in-law?" Bianca asked.

"It's too soon for the coroner to release the cause of death," Tory told her.

I got a bad feeling. Suppose the knife turned up with Wes's blood on it? Even if it hadn't struck the fatal blow, that could be damning.

Tory maintained her composure. "Barry gave it to Dad to return to you. I'll ask what he did with it. Since he didn't hand it to you, he either still has it or he put it somewhere obvious."

"Obvious to whom?" Noah grumbled.

I was wondering the same thing. And that raised another consideration. While the killer had targeted Wes, was Parker merely a convenient scapegoat or was there a reason to want them both out of the way?

Tory didn't waste time on speculation. Practical as ever, she said, "Describe the knife, please."

Parker gazed at us wistfully. "It's one of those folding utility gizmos with a corkscrew, can opener, and screw driver. I miss it."

"Anything to identify it as yours?"

"It's engraved with my initials."

"Perfect. That will tell the police who to blame." Irritably, Bianca fumbled in her pocket. When her husband glared, she withdrew her hand, empty.

She must have a serious habit if she required another cigarette this soon. In fairness, though, how often does your family get caught up in a murder investigation?

"Whoever used your phone might also have stolen the knife," Tory said. "Tell your lawyer about it and let him decide what to tell the police. "

"Don't reveal any more than you absolutely have to," Bianca warned.

That concluded the meeting. Probing homicides wasn't part of my medical training, I reflected as we took our leave, but through my sister-in-law and through unfortunate circumstances, I was getting an education all the same.

"They made an odd choice of attorney," Tory commented when we reached her car.

"How's that?"

"Joseph Noriega's reputable. But he isn't the kind of shark rich people usually hire when they're in trouble."

"You know him?" I asked as we pulled away from the curb.

"I've done a few jobs for Joseph." As a PI, she often assisted

53

attorneys with their cases. "He's competent, yes. Brilliant, no."

To the best of my knowledge, the Bryerlys had had little or nothing to do with criminal matters until now. The advantages of engaging a shark probably hadn't occurred to them. "They hired you. That was smart."

"I'm betting I have Parker to thank for that," she said. "By the way, did Cress tell you anything about her husband's side of the family?"

"A little." I filled in my sister-in-law about the alcoholic parents and the ID-stealing sibling.

"I'll check them out." She rounded the corner onto our street. "I haven't found any criminal record for the deceased. Not under the name Westlake Choate."

"You think he was using a false name?" I doubted I'd ever develop a police officer's mistrustful instincts.

Tory shrugged. "He could have changed it to distance himself from that family. But it's a long shot. Oh, good. Looks like I won't have to go far for my next interview."

Ahead, a white van with gold trim occupied the curb in front of my house. The brown lettering read Golden Fine Foods Catering.

My father-in-law, the last person in possession of Parker's knife, was home.

*

"Murder makes me nervous." Short and balding with puffs of gray hair above his ears, Morris Golden positioned a baking dish atop a trivet on the kitchen counter. Choppy movements testified to his agitation.

He had reason to be on edge. At Sunday night's dinner party, he'd most likely had a brush with a murderer, since whoever had sent that text must have been on the premises.

"Morris has been a-flutter all day." His catering assistant, an energetic, seventyish widow named Helen Pepper, set a bowl of pilaf beside the eggplant-and-tomato casserole. "Being hauled down to the police station didn't improve his mood."

"Keith interviewed you?" I asked.

"No, that other detective. Horner." Morris returned his oven mitts to a peg. "He's a—what's the phrase kids use? Total douche."

He had to be highly provoked to use that kind of language. Even Tory, absorbed in prying a paper plate from the stack, looked mildly shocked.

"Oh! I forgot the salad." From the refrigerator, Helen retrieved a large glass bowl. Although off duty after delivering dinners to clients, she still wore her uniform, a black apron over a white shirt and black trousers. It set off her silver hair.

Until recently, the former homemaker had told me, arthritis had reduced her to semi-invalid status. Rescued by new medication, she'd leaped at the chance to work for Morris and, as she put it, re-enter the world.

Helen didn't need the income. Her late daughter's second husband had been a billionaire equity investor, and after the couple died in a car crash two years earlier, she'd become executor of their trust. She also shared guardianship of her two teenage granddaughters with their father, an anesthesiologist friend of mine.

Morris joined Tory and me at the table. "Have they figured out who killed Wes?"

"Dad, they just discovered the body this morning."

Morris clenched and unclenched his hands. "The police kept asking me who was at the Bryerlys' dinner."

"Who was, exactly?" Tory, I presumed, was double-checking what her clients had told us.

Morris cited the same names we'd heard earlier. "That detective harped on whether I'd borrowed somebody else's phone. Why would I do that when I can hardly figure out how to use mine?"

"I wish I'd been there." Helen looked up from eating a small salad at the counter. "I love trying to guess who dunnit on TV."

"Don't take those shows too seriously," I said. Keith often complained about the inaccuracies, such as cops failing to separate witnesses. Still, he couldn't seem to resist watching.

"Don't spoil my fun." Helen winked.

"It was no fun being grilled, let me tell you," Morris complained.

"Anyone mention a knife?" Tory asked.

Her father perked up. "The Bryerlys have a wonderful set of German blades. Fantastic how they hold an edge."

"I meant Parker's pocket knife," she said. "Weren't you supposed to return it for Barry?"

"Yes, but I didn't get a chance to talk to him, so I left it on a side table." Morris's jaw worked. "I forgot to tell Parker it was there. Oh, my gosh! Is that what... was that how...?"

"It's missing," I told him. "Maybe it fell on the floor."

"If it did, Agatha would have picked it up," my father-in-law said. "Or did the killer take it? Oh, dear, oh, dear. What have I done?"

"It might not mean anything," Tory assured him.

"But if I lost it, I should replace it."

"That's Barry's responsibility," she assured him. "You were doing him a favor."

For a few minutes, we digested this, and our meals, in silence. Then Helen spoke. "I wish I'd insisted the girls sign up for the second session of sports camp."

Since this remark came out of the blue, no one responded. Finally I asked, "Why?"

"My granddaughters spent the entire morning glued to the window fighting over a pair of binoculars," she explained. "They texted me every detail of what the police and coroner

56

did. That can't be healthy."

Now I understood. The girls lived in the same house where Keely rented a room. It belonged to their stepmother, who'd been taking in renters since before she married their dad. All of which meant the girls, who were on summer vacation, had had a front-row seat to the crime scene.

"Are they upset?" I asked.

"I don't think so," Helen said. "They love cop shows, too."

"Well, I'm upset." Morris had barely touched his meal.

His daughter patted his hand. "Try not to dwell on it, Dad."

"How do I avoid that?"

"Invent new recipes."

"Ah." His expression warmed. "I *have* been meaning to experiment with artichokes."

I hoped we'd finished discussing the crime. With luck, the police would soon learn that Wes had been killed by a loan shark or someone he'd tried to blackmail with a photograph. That would let my patients and my neighbors off the hook.

Helen, however, hadn't had her fill of couch detecting. "Do you suppose he was murdered because of that surrogate?"

"No!" I snapped. "For what possible reason?"

"Jealousy," she suggested. "I mean, if she has a boyfriend, he might resent her carrying another man's child."

"Surrogacies don't involve sex." *At least, they aren't supposed to.* "There's no reason for jealousy toward the intended father." Also, Tanya had insisted she wasn't dating anyone, information I didn't share because it was private.

"You did bypass the hospital's normal requirements," Tory remarked.

"Those requirements are for commercial surrogates." Hearing the irritation in my tone, I took a deep breath before continuing, "Tanya is a friend of the wife's. She volunteered."

"How generous of her." Helen studied me thoughtfully.

"What motivates commercial surrogates? Are they just in it for the money?"

Although childbirth today is far, far safer than in earlier ages, with life-threatening complications arising in less than one percent of cases, death or serious injury still occurs. In my opinion, money alone is never enough to compensate a woman.

"Not entirely, although it's only fair they get paid," I said. "Often, they enjoy being pregnant and are thrilled to provide a family with a longed-for child. But they spend many hours on doctor visits, plus the actual birth and recovery. If there are complications, they may have to take leave from their regular jobs."

"How much do they typically charge?" Tory asked.

"Upwards of twenty thousand dollars." While I didn't deal with the financial side of surrogacy, I had to be prepared with general information for my patients.

"I admire them," Helen said. "Giving birth was so painful, I decided to stop at one child."

"I'd stop at none." Tory went for a second helping. She gets bored whenever the conversation touches on motherhood.

Helen wasn't finished, however. "Mind if I ask you a question?"

"You already did," Morris said.

"I mean, medical advice, of a sort."

"That depends." *Please don't describe symptoms.* Dinner-table diagnoses are a bad idea, not to mention unappetizing.

"When my daughter and her husband died, they'd been undergoing fertility treatments," Helen said. "I'm responsible for their frozen embryos. I hate to discard them. What are my options?"

That was a tricky subject. Many people regard the embryos as children, in which case disposing of them or donating them to research would be offensive.

"You can donate them to an infertile couple, or commission a surrogate." I assumed the trust fund could cover the expenses. That didn't resolve who would raise the children, of course. "Frozen embryos can be stored for many years."

She rose and began clearing plates. "I'm glad there's no hurry."

"Can we talk about something else now?" Tory asked.

Helen smiled. "How about that nurse's birthday party Friday night? It should be fun."

"A laugh riot." Judging by Tory's expression, she'd almost rather return to the subject of babies.

Too late. Morris, whom Narda had hired to cater, was happy to review menu and serving options with his assistant. Even Tory offered a few suggestions, clearly pleased to see her father in a better mood.

So was I. Parties. Babies. Happy things. I leaned back with eyes half shut, drifting closer to contentment than I had in several days.

I should have known better.

CHAPTER SEVEN

"I can't believe that photographer went and got himself killed right behind my house," Keely sniffed on Wednesday morning as we entered the crowded elevator in the medical office building. "Just imagine! What're his wife and that surrogate going to do?"

Although Keely is both my housekeeper and another obstetrician's nurse, I'm not permitted to discuss patients with her. Nor did I care to participate in gossip. Instead, recalling Helen's concern about her binoculars-wielding granddaughters, I asked, "Has your home settled back to normal yet?"

Ignoring the other staffers squeezed around us, Keely snorted. "Hah! It's a good thing houses don't tip over like boats from people running to one side to stare."

"Why?" asked a nurse's aide as the doors thudded shut. "What's up?"

"Murder most foul," Keely said. "Right in my back yard."

"Really?"

The question went unanswered. At the second floor, Keely exited. En route to the fourth floor, I ignored curious glances and wished I'd taken the stairs.

There was no escaping the buzz, however. That morning, *The Safe Harbor Journal* had headlined the discovery of Westlake Choate's body. Its star reporter did her best to spice things up by stating that Wes was renowned for his sensual art photography. She'd also raked up Noah Bryerly's history of selling out his hugely successful software business and retiring an early age, implying the family must be a hotbed of pleasure-seeking.

The truth was far less colorful, according to a profile of him I'd searched out last night. It said he enjoyed traveling with his wife and had invested in a range of firms, most recently a company producing sports drinks and health foods. As for why he hadn't continued to develop software, he claimed he'd simply lost interest.

Once immersed in patient care, I set other matters aside. At midday, eating a sandwich at my desk, I put in calls to patients who'd been experiencing problems. This provides reassurance, reinforces my instructions, and helps pinpoint issues before they become critical.

It bothered me that I couldn't reach Maggie Majors, the patient on bed rest, who epitomized the type of altruistic paid surrogate I'd described to Helen. Maggie didn't pick up her cell phone or her land line.

I tried the intended mother, Danielle Jeffers. No response there either.

"Dr. Darcy?" My nurse, Farrah Ortiz, appeared in the doorway. A tall, well-groomed woman in her early thirties, she often ate lunch in our staff room. Although she had every right to go out to eat, I appreciated her sticking around as backup. "You have a visitor."

I felt a spurt of hope that it might be the missing Maggie. Instead, Farrah ushered in my buddy. Although Keith's suit was wilting from the August heat, that only emphasized his broad shoulders, which my nurse was studying appreciatively.

It occurred to me that he had, to the best of my recollection, never before visited me at work. I wondered what he thought of the place. Not that an obstetrician's office is much different from any other doctor's aside from the type of magazines and the children's play area in the waiting room.

"Hey, there." I rounded the desk to shake hands. Rather formal, but Farrah was watching. So, I realized, was Glenda Glover, our young receptionist, who moved to the side where she could presumably enjoy Keith's rugged appeal.

In her early twenties, Glenda is single, while Farrah's divorced. My employees' romantic status isn't a subject to which I normally pay attention. Neither did Keith, a fact they must have noted, because they vanished in a cloud of disappointment.

"What brings you here?" I asked.

"I'd like to review your discovery of the body," he said. "Anything else you've remembered. Or that might not have made it into the initial report."

"Fine." I sat behind my desk. With patients, I occupy a guest chair, to avoid putting a barrier between us. However, I noted the disdain that flickered across my friend's face as he observed my framed credentials and diplomas, including one from Harvard Medical School.

Although Keith has several degrees, including a masters in criminal justice, he dislikes the arrogance he associates with doctors. We come by our attitudes the old-fashioned way: I'm the son of an OB/GYN and he's the son of a small-town police chief.

Today, I chose to maintain my professional distance.

With my permission, he activated his voice recorder and started with the date, hour, place, his introduction and my name, which he asked me to state so a transcriber could identify my voice. "Let's review what you were doing on Pelican Lane."

I repeated what I'd told the officer at the scene: jogging, noticing the birds, recalling Keely's remark about howling coyotes, and putting that together with Wes's car being found at the harbor.

"Who told you about that?" he demanded.

"Mrs. Bryerly. The elderly one." I explained how I'd encountered Lenore. For good measure, I repeated her suspicion that when her husband drowned eight years earlier, there'd been someone else in the boat.

"Did she say who?"

"No."

"You think this is connected?" Keith asked.

"Not necessarily. She suffers from dementia," I said. "I'm just telling you what happened."

"She say anything else?"

In the interest of full disclosure, I repeated, "Her great-granddaughter, Wes's wife, is unhappy, according to her. And she accused me of putting their surrogate right in the middle, without specifying the middle of what. Have you interviewed Lenore?"

He didn't answer. Typical; Keith never shares details of an investigation. While he jotted notes, I checked my phone. No missed calls and no message from Maggie or Danielle.

Keith spoke again. "Tell me what Tory's learned from the Bryerlys."

"Why don't you ask her?" I said.

"She owes them her discretion. You don't."

"Actually, I do," I said. "Their daughter is my patient."

That didn't require me to keep quiet about Parker's missing knife. However, while I'd never hide vital information from the police, this might be irrelevant. Or, my instincts nagged, part of the killer's attempt to frame an innocent man.

After a moment, Keith continued. "Speaking of the daughter, she and the victim commissioned a surrogate, correct?"

Although that information was well known, I wasn't comfortable confirming it. "Did she tell you that?"

He failed to suppress a sigh. "How much does that cost?"

"Depends." In more detail than I'd provided to Morris's assistant, I sketched the range of expenses involved in a surrogacy. These can run over one hundred thousand dollars when you include in vitro fertilization, legal fees, medical coverage, out-of-pocket reimbursements such as for maternity clothes, and payment to the surrogate.

"Using this woman, Tanya Nichols, saved a lot of that, right?" Keith said.

"No doubt."

"But it's still expensive. Who's paying for it?"

"You should ask Cress."

He waited again, in case silence might prompt me to ramble on. When that failed, he asked, "What about the relationship between the deceased and Ms. Nichols?"

"They must have been on good terms," I said. "Wes photographed her as the pregnancy progressed."

"Naked?"

"In the photos he showed me, she wore a bikini," I answered. "You should check with the Wine Arts Gallery. There's an exhibit of Wes's pictures scheduled to open Sunday."

"I'll have Detective Horner talk to the owner." Art galleries aren't high on Keith's list of favorite spots to visit.

I peered at my phone again.

"What's so damn important?"

"Worried about a patient," I said. "Not related."

"Would you tell me if it was?"

"No."

He grimaced. It must have been a long few days, dealing with the heat, the wetlands, the witnesses and the press. Nevertheless, that goes with the job. I didn't expect his sympathy when I was summoned for middle-of-the-night deliveries.

Keith concluded the interview with the time and deactivated the recorder. "Got another question for you," he said. "Off the subject."

I welcomed a change. "Shoot."

"Narda keeps hinting she expects a special present for her birthday, and I can't figure out what to buy," he said. "I never had to worry about this kind of thing with Tory. She likes the same stuff I do."

That intrigued me. "What would you have given Tory?"

"A set of personalized beer mugs." Judging by Keith's faraway expression, he was picturing either a beer or my sister-in-law. "No, better—a laser-guided pizza cutter. That would be cool."

"I'll buy you one for Christmas."

"Gee, thanks."

"Definitely not special enough for Narda's birthday," I said. Turning thirty is a watershed moment for most of us, although the change of decades hadn't bothered me. I'd been happy that year: finishing my residency, planning to practice alongside my father and anticipating a loving future with my wife. "How about jewelry? If you can find a piece with a Greek theme, that might do the trick."

"Like a sorority pin?"

"Not if you value your life." How had he reached the age of thirty-six without more insight into women's tastes? "Like a necklace." Receiving a blank stare, I said, "There's an artisan site called Etsy. Do a search for Greek jewelry."

"Thanks." Keith got to his feet. Asking for advice bothered him, I could tell. He hates being in a subordinate position.

When his mocking gaze once again swept the wall documents, I braced for a parting shot. Here it came. "Doesn't it feel weird, doing what you do?"

"In what sense?"

"All these women. Every day. Looking up their..." He left the sentence unfinished.

The remark irked me. "Women visit me for help, not to fulfill my puerile curiosity and certainly not to be snickered at."

"I didn't mean that."

To hell with his half-hearted apology. "What I do here is save lives. My mother didn't consult a doctor when she should have. Maybe being married to one made her over-confident, or maybe it was because she ate organic vegetables and used only natural products. She figured checkups weren't necessary, and by the time she found the lump, the cancer had spread. Or perhaps she was just embarrassed to have a doctor look up her whatever."

"Eric, I wasn't thinking." Regret shaded his eyes. He knew how rarely I lost my temper.

I struggled to stem the torrent of memories. The frustration and anguish for two years as Dad and I watched Mom be injected with poison in an effort to stop the monster. The suffering and the fighting, to no avail. I'd spent my junior high years riding a roller coaster of hope and grief. If only she'd gone in earlier. If only...

Take a deep breath, Eric.

Keith wasn't to blame. If anything, he'd saved me during that miserable period when I'd been a skinny nerd. The big guy had needed my help to pass his math and science courses, and I'd needed his to fend off bullies.

"Forget it," I said. "You hit a nerve."

"I noticed."

His cell rang. At almost the same moment, so did mine.

It occurred to me this might stem from some emergency that affected us both, until I saw the name Danielle Jeffers on the screen. I took the call at once.

"I'm at the hospital with Maggie." She sounded anxious. "She's in labor. Can you come over?"

"I'll be right there." Labor in a patient with placenta previa required immediate attention. I clicked off, mentally preparing an apology to my nurse for the inevitable delays in the afternoon schedule. "Gotta go, Keith."

"Me, too. They found the murder weapon." He blinked. "I didn't say that."

"Understood." I nearly asked if it was a knife and if it had initials on it. But he wouldn't have told me, anyway.

I suspected I'd find out soon enough.

CHAPTER EIGHT

One of the great philosophical questions is whether, as we travel through life, we encounter people for a reason or purely by chance. I suppose it's possible both things are true: that we're surrounded by random crowds but from them, in some subtle manner, we draw or are drawn to key individuals.

As I hurried into Maggie's room in Labor and Delivery, I thought of this not in the context of my relationship with Keith but because standing at the foot of her bed was a physician who had been an unwelcome part of my social and professional sphere since medical school. Tall and bony with a long nose and penetrating dark eyes, Dr. Jeremiah Schwartz graced me with a collegial nod.

"I have examined the patient and ordered an ultrasound. I trust you will approve." Although he hailed from New York, Jeremiah spoke English stiffly, as if it were his second language. "Celia alerted me while I was in the cafeteria."

Celia, his office nurse, was the sister of the intended mother, Danielle. She had also donated the egg that resulted in the soon-to-arrive baby.

Taking the proffered clipboard, I assessed the situation. The mother was slightly dilated, which indicated this was true labor. At thirty-four weeks, the baby would be viable, but the lungs might not yet be mature.

Nurses had started an IV and hooked up the fetal monitor. Maggie lay propped on the pillows, her skin pale. Danielle, chair pulled to the bed, was patting the surrogate's free arm.

I'm accustomed to having another doctor step in if a patient arrives at night or on a weekend. However, I'd been only a few minutes away. In fact, I suspected I'd have been notified sooner had Jeremiah not inserted himself into the case. "I wish you'd waited for me."

"My apologies," he said.

Since he didn't sound terribly sorry, I didn't bother to pardon him. "Maggie, how are you feeling?"

"Scared," she admitted. "I didn't have this kind of trouble before."

"Every pregnancy is different." Plus she was eight years older now than when she'd previously given birth. "Tell me what happened."

Labor pains had begun that morning. While she talked, I checked the fetal heart rate, which was normal, and noted that, at this stage, the little one had an excellent chance of surviving and thriving.

"We should have called you immediately," Maggie said.

"We weren't thinking straight," Danielle put in. "Celia's a nurse, so I called her."

"No harm done." Patients tend to blame themselves for what are simply human reactions. "The important thing is that Maggie's in the hospital. There's a good chance we can get this under control. Every day the baby stays inside is a plus."

I prescribed medication to stop labor and speed the maturation of the baby's lungs, and promised to return later. When I left, Jeremiah shadowed me to the elevator.

"Fascinating," he said as we waited in the hall. "I had not

thought about the fact that a surrogacy is treated like any other pregnancy."

What a bizarre comment for an obstetrician. Except for Jeremiah. Despite an acquaintance stretching back more than a dozen years, I never knew what he would say or do next.

A few highlights: during medical school, when Lydia and I briefly broke up, Jeremiah had swooped in to date her. They'd had little in common, as far as I could tell, aside from both being grandchildren of Holocaust survivors.

After she and I reconciled, I thought for a while he was stalking us. He'd unexpectedly chosen to do his residency alongside me at the University of California, Irvine, and leased an office in my medical building as soon as one became available. He even bought a car identical to mine.

Yet neither Lydia nor I ever saw him near our house, nor did he contact us outside work. While I believed he was in love with her, the disturbing parallels continued after her death. When I traded my hybrid for an electric car, he did the same, special-ordering the identical color.

I didn't exactly feel threatened. Mostly annoyed.

"You've never treated a surrogate?" I asked.

"I have not." Jeremiah bent his knees as if to minimize his four-inch height advantage over me. "I did not realize it was such a large part of your practice."

"Not that large." I saw a range of women, including older patients inherited from my father, like Lenore Bryerly.

"Celia has explained how rewarding it was to donate eggs for her sister," he continued. "She said that it brings the family closer."

"Having a baby by any means tends to bring a family closer," I said as the elevator arrived.

"So I am learning." He waited politely, then followed me into the empty lift.

I seemed to be sharing a lot of conversations in elevators these days, I mused. At least this one contained no eavesdroppers.

When the doors closed, I asked something I had wondered for years. "Jeremiah, why did you specialize in obstetrics?"

He shrugged as if the answer were obvious. "Because you did."

"That's the only reason?"

"It seemed a sensible thing to do."

As I said, I never knew what would pop out of his mouth.

Wednesday afternoon flew by. I stayed late to catch up with patients, then looked in on Maggie. Resting comfortably without further contractions, she agreed to stay in the hospital for a few days. If there were no problems, she could then resume bed rest at home.

Events had pushed Wes's murder to the back of my mind, but in my car, I thought about the stress it must be placing on Tanya. Only a few weeks from her due date, she could deliver at any time. So far, her blood pressure had been normal, but the situation was unusual, to say the least.

I pressed her number in my cell, mounted on the dashboard. When she answered, she sounded breathless. "Eric, I'm glad you phoned."

"What's wrong?" I asked. "Do you need to come in?"

"Physically, I'm fine," the surrogate told me. "But..." Speaking to someone else, she said, "No, that photo shoot is a week from Saturday. Please speak to the bride directly. I don't know what she had in mind." Back to me: "Cress arranged for this photographer, Duncan Axelrod, to handle Wes's assignments. I'm bringing him up to speed."

The name stirred an image of a chunky, earnest fellow I'd seen at a few weddings. "That's fine. But you should take it easy."

"I can't." Tanya sighed. "Keith and a guy from the coroner's office told Cress this morning that the cause of death was a stab wound. She completely freaked out. It was bad enough to know Wes died, but worse to learn the gory details."

A stab wound. With a knife like Parker's? But the authorities wouldn't release that much detail. "Was anyone with her?"

"I was down here in the studio. I ran upstairs when she called."

Running on stairs was unwise, especially in her condition. However, nagging after the fact wouldn't be helpful, either, so I refrained. "Her parents aren't around?"

"Are you kidding? Not them. Parker's been in touch by phone. Someone advised him not to stop by in person."

Yes, I recalled that. "Did the police say anything else?"

"Just that Wes put up a fight. Whoever did this must have bruises."

I hadn't noticed marks on Parker or anyone else. "How is Cress?"

"She's sleeping. She took that sedative you prescribed."

Understandable, considering the circumstances. "What about you? Any dizziness? Nausea? Abdominal pain?"

"No," Tanya answered. "All the same, it's good to talk to you, Eric. I feel better touching bases with someone sane."

"That's what I'm here for." I crested the hill overlooking the harbor. "Call me if you have any symptoms or need a shoulder to lean on."

"I will," she promised.

A minute later, the phone rang. Tory wasted no time on pleasantries. "Are you home? Is Dad with you?"

"I'm in the car, on final approach." I was winding through quiet residential streets. At well past seven p.m., despite lingering traces of daylight, the world felt deserted. "What's up?"

"Helen's worried." Tory huffed impatiently. "The police interrupted while she and Dad were delivering meals. They wanted him at the station immediately for further questioning. No explanation."

My mind flicked back to my conversation with Keith. "They found the murder weapon."

"Parker's knife?"

"Possibly. The cause of death was a stab wound." And my father-in-law had been the last person to admit possessing the knife. "Why is Helen worried?"

"It's been nearly two hours. She tried to reach him about tomorrow's schedule but he didn't answer, and I can't get hold of him, either. According to the desk sergeant, Dad left the station a while ago."

"He probably forgot to turn his phone back on after the interview." Morris was uncomfortable managing the device. He still occasionally asked my help entering new contacts.

"Maybe."

"I thought you attached a GPS device to his truck." Her abundance of caution had paid off in the past.

"He lost it."

"How do you lose a GPS device?"

"Dad's gifted," she grumbled. "I'm on my way to his office. Can you check the house?" Tory doesn't panic easily, but the last time Morris vanished, he'd turned out to be in deadly danger.

"Will do." As long as I had her on the line, I asked, "If it *is* Parker's knife, will they arrest him? Parker, I mean, not your dad." I had more respect for the district attorney's office than to believe they'd target my father-in-law.

"Depends on whether the D.A. believes there's enough evidence to convict," she said. "Can they persuade a jury that a computer scientist, obviously tech-savvy, texted from his personal phone to set up a murder and left his engraved knife near the scene?"

"People do stupid things." And brilliant people can be arrogant. But that wasn't my impression of Parker. "But I'll... Oh, bloody hell!" As I turned onto my street, I forgot Tory and everything else.

Careening toward me, the Golden Fine Foods truck swerved wildly. At the wheel, Morris had the wide-eyed stare of a man frightened out of his senses.

CHAPTER NINE

I hit the horn and jerked my car to the side. Snapping out of his daze, Morris crunched to the opposite curb. He sat there motionless, gripping the wheel.

"What? What?" Tory yelled over my phone.

"Your father nearly hit me. He's fine. We're both fine. More later." Pulling the cell from its holder, I ran to the catering truck. "Morris?" He didn't stir. "Talk to me!"

"There's someone in the back of the van." The puffs of gray hair over his ears were standing on end. "I've been trying to shake him. Is he still there? Be careful! He might have a gun."

"Get out." I yanked on the driver's door. Fumblingly, Morris unlocked it and climbed down.

"Stand clear." As I dialed 911, I circled on the sidewalk. If anyone remained in the vehicle, I had no intention of putting myself in his path. Neither did I intend to let him escape unseen.

The rear doors gaped open, revealing rows of empty shelves designed to hold hot boxes. There was enough space, narrowly, for a person to squeeze in behind them, but I didn't see how anyone could have broken through to the front seat and attacked Morris.

Even if he hadn't been in immediate danger, it must have been terrifying to hear a person shifting around. What had the intruder been doing?

I didn't doubt my father-in-law's perceptions. While he may overreact on occasion, I believed he'd heard something or someone moving around.

I was explaining the situation to the dispatcher when the shrubbery stirred on the slope that connects Sunset Circle to the street above. Whoever had fled the truck might be fleeing along the footpath.

"There's movement in the bushes," I told the dispatcher. "I'm going after him."

"Sir, please don't confront an armed suspect," she said. "An officer will be there in two minutes."

"I'll just try to keep him in sight," I promised.

"Don't be a hero."

"No danger of that."

On the sidewalk, Morris stood twisting his hands. "I must have forgotten to lock the van while I was in the station. Do you think it's the killer? Is he after me?"

"He's gone. Call your daughter," I told him, and raced toward the footpath.

There, I discovered that the person ruffling the bushes wasn't the fleeing suspect. Instead, Lenore Bryerly tottered down toward me, leaning on a twisted cane.

"Dennis, hello." She raised a gnarly hand in greeting.

"Did you see a man running away?" I demanded.

She shook her cloud of white hair. "Honey, I heard tires screech. There isn't a fire, is there?"

Squealing tires don't normally bring to mind a fire, even in Southern California's dry season, when the slightest spark can ignite a blaze. "No, Mrs. Bryerly," I assured her, scanning the street but spotting nothing of interest. "Are you certain no one passed you?"

She frowned. "There's no fire?"

Despite my impatience, I reminded myself that Lenore's confusion wasn't her fault. "Only an uninvited hitchhiker."

"Fires scare me ever since I found out how they died," the old lady said.

I dredged up more patience. "Since who died?"

"The fire that killed my daughter and her young man."

She was referring to Noah's parents, but what did their long-ago deaths have to do with anything? "Mrs. Bryerly, you should head home."

"We didn't hear about it for ages," she rambled on. "Saul and I thought Georgette was gallivanting around all that while. We didn't recover our darling Noah until a couple of years later."

On my street, a cruiser with a flashing light bar pulled to a halt. "I'm afraid I'm needed elsewhere. Oh, here's your helper."

Agatha huffed down toward us, trailing a multicolored scarf. "Thank goodness she's with you, Dr. Darcy. I wish she wouldn't do this."

"People with her condition tend to wander," I said.

Sadness pinched Lenore's thin face. "My daughter wandered too far," she said. "Poor Georgie. Do y'all think we were bad parents?"

"Of course not." I allowed Agatha to take her arm. "Mrs. Bryerly, please forgive me. I have to go."

"I understand." Her mouth trembled.

In front of my house, Morris was telling a skeptical uniformed officer about the intruder. When Tory joined us, the cop ignored her. He wrote down my name, however.

I'd encountered Officer Ochs and his attitude before. He seemed to believe that when Tory left the force, she'd cast herself into the outer darkness.

"You didn't actually see anyone?" he asked Morris.

"No, officer."

"Did you, Dr. Darcy?"

I conceded that I hadn't. "Only an elderly neighbor curious about the fuss."

"I'll log an incident report. Thank you."

Tory glared. "You should fingerprint the van!"

His expression stopped barely short of a sneer. "Yeah, okay." A few minutes later, after doing a half-hearted job, Ochs got back in the cruiser.

"Assbite," Tory muttered. "Dad, I can park the van for you."

"I'll do it." My father-in-law sucked in a deep breath and, sure enough, accomplished the task unaided, with only a few jerky motions.

When he joined us indoors, he still appeared distraught. Tory tucked him into bed with a glass of warm milk.

"How is he?" I set my plate of leftovers on the counter.

"He's watching his favorite show, *Dogs With Jobs*. That should calm him." Tory slapped together a sandwich.

"Care to speculate who was in the van?" I'd drawn a blank.

My sister-in-law brought her food and a beer to the stool beside me. "Whoever it was probably sneaked into the van outside the police station. Might be a guy who just got out of jail and was looking to steal valuables. They're releasing a lot of so-called nonviolent offenders these days, thanks to our government's commitment to saving money by sacrificing law-abiding citizens."

Since this was a familiar rant, I moved on. "Learn anything new about the case today?"

She took a swig of beer. "I confirmed what you told me about Wes's background."

"He didn't change his name to hide a criminal record?" I was only half joking.

78

"Not as far as I can tell," she responded. "Also, there's no indication he had received threats."

"What kind of threats would you expect?"

"From a jealous husband or a blackmail victim," Tory said. "I'm sure a handsome photographer can find numerous ways to get into trouble."

She sounded tired. It was hard not to think of Tory as the kid who'd trailed Lydia and me through high school, the gawky youngster who'd zoomed up to five-foot-ten and, uncertain where her body began and ended, ran into open locker doors and dropped her books on my feet. She was thirty-three, not exactly middle-aged but en route. Today, it showed.

"Who were you talking to on the slope?" she asked.

"Lenore Bryerly."

"What was she doing out there? She's what, ninety-five?"

"Ninety-six." I reviewed the conversation. "She mentioned that her daughter and the boyfriend—I gather they weren't married—died in a fire when Noah was a kid. She and Saul didn't learn about it for a couple of years."

"Why did she bring that up?"

Despite Lenore's dementia, I respected the emotions behind her seemingly disjointed statements. "Wes's death has stirred up painful memories, like her husband Saul's drowning eight years ago. In her mind, everything's connected."

Tory tilted her head as she considered the matter. "They used to live in Texas, right?"

"Yes. They moved out here about nine years ago," I said.

"Why?"

"To be closer to family, I guess." It had been a fatal decision, although only by accident. Or *was* there a link between Wes's and Saul's deaths? "Parker must have been in his early twenties when his great-grandfather drowned."

"Why does that matter?" Tory asked.

"Suppose he was in the boat when Saul fell overboard? Maybe they fought and the family covered it up."

"And now Lenore's dropping hints?" she murmured. "Might indicate a guilty conscience for betraying her husband by staying silent. Or suppressed anger at her great-grandson. If she blames him for her husband's death, she might be trying to finger him for Wes's, too."

Was I wrong to believe in Parker's innocence? His alibi left wiggle room, and it was hard to account for the text message from his phone. Still, anger about Wes cheating on his sister hardly struck me as a motive for murder.

"I can't imagine what Keith was thinking, grilling Dad about that knife," Tory went on. "In my opinion, he's overdoing the tough guy act to show how impartial he is. And maybe punish me a little for dumping him."

Even though Keith's machismo comment about my patients had angered me, I respected my friend's professionalism. "He has a murder to solve. He can't play favorites."

"And how could he let my father drive home, all upset like that?" Tory went on.

"You can't blame Keith for someone sneaking into the van."

"Maybe not, but he should have known Dad was too agitated to drive safely. Even Lydia used to say Dad was so vulnerable, she felt protective toward him."

Her statement struck me as off somehow. Finally, I figured out which word didn't ring true. "What do you mean, *even* Lydia?" My wife had been kind-hearted. Not uncritical, true; she'd had high standards, and sharp words for anyone she considered a fool, but she'd loved her family. Including Morris.

Tory gnawed a cuticle. "She always referred to him as her stepfather. Never her father or her dad. Why not? He raised her. She barely knew her own father."

"She felt a strong bond to him." Lydia had told me about

Avram Silver, who, according to her mother, had suffered recurring bouts of depression and committed suicide when she was three. His parents—her grandparents—had survived the Holocaust but suffered from despair and survivor's guilt. They'd died in Israel when Avram was young, although my wife hadn't known the specifics. In her darker moods, she'd identified with him, and perhaps them, too.

"It didn't matter that Dad was there for us, that he loved her since she was a toddler?" Tory's words had a late-in-a-long-day raggedness. "And she used to introduce me as her half-sister rather than her sister. Why did she hold me at arm's length? I practically idolized her."

"Are you seriously asking?"

"Do you seriously have an answer? Eric, did she share something with you?"

She had, in confidence. But Lydia was dead, and she no longer owned her secrets. "Count backwards," I said.

"Why?"

"How long before your birth did your parents get married?"

Tory's shoulders sagged. "Yeah, I figured that out. Mom was pregnant already. So what?"

"How long after Avram Silver's death were your parents married?"

She stared at me, as if not quite willing to deal with this aspect of her history. "It was pretty quick. A few months."

"Keep counting."

I pictured reels spinning in her brain and awareness slotting into place. "Mom got pregnant with me while her first husband was alive," Tory said slowly. "Eric, Avram Silver wasn't my father. Dad wouldn't have lied to me all these years."

"Lydia didn't doubt that Morris is your father."

"She thought he and Mom had been having an affair?" She closed her eyes. "Is that what pushed her father over the

81

edge?"

I wished I didn't have to share the rest, but we'd gone too far. "He left a suicide note. He was already depressed, and when she cheated, he decided she'd be happier without him." A curious child, Lydia had run across the note while snooping through her mother's drawers. Later, it had vanished, probably destroyed by her mom.

Nelle Golden had been an energetic woman with an imperious manner. A talented interior designer, she'd succeeded with the aid of a great color sense and a perfectionist nature. I'd never felt comfortable around her, although she'd approved of me. Her death in a car crash when Lydia was twenty-three had devastated her family.

"Oh, God." Tory pressed a hand to her forehead.

I hate family secrets. They cause terrible pain and tend to emerge at crisis points that magnify their impact. "I'm sorry."

Tears glazed her eyes. "To Lydia, I guess I was living proof of their betrayal."

That seemed harsh. "She loved you."

"Not as much as I loved her."

At this sensitive moment, the doorbell rang. Tory flinched. "Who the hell is that?"

"I'll get it."

On the porch stood an excited Narda, arms full of glittering decorations. An exhausted Keith, the lines in his forehead deeper than usual, supported a giant cardboard statue of a Greek god.

I'd forgotten that Narda, who had Wednesdays free, had requested my permission to decorate for the party tonight, two days in advance. She must have nagged or pressured Keith into accompanying her, despite being in the middle of a murder investigation.

He didn't appear happy about it. And in view of the

bombshell Tory had just received, things were likely to go downhill, fast.

"Well, here you are," I said, and, seeing no reasonable alternative, let them in.

CHAPTER TEN

Tory shot to her feet as we approached. Our conversation about Lydia must have knocked down her personal firewall, because she glared at our guests as if they were invading viruses.

"Oh, bloody hell!" she burst out, and stalked up the stairs.

"What did we do?" Narda asked me.

"She's had a rough day."

Keith plunked the mock statue onto the floor. "We all have. So what?"

Narda set her armload on a sofa in the great room. There were rolls of gold gossamer, packets of balloons, golden ribbons and a shopping bag filled with trinkets.

"She's upset about Morris," I said. That was true enough. Besides, the shock Tory had just received was none of his or Narda's business.

"I had to question him," Keith said. "That would be obvious if she didn't have a stick up her..."

"I meant afterwards."

"What afterwards?"

The incident had gone down only an hour ago. Clearly, neither Officer Ochs nor the watch commander had informed him.

As I described the intruder in the catering truck, thumping noises issued from upstairs. Tory was working off her frustrations on my exercise equipment.

"Is Morris all right?" Keith glanced toward the closed door of the downstairs bedroom.

"Settled in front of the TV," I replied.

"You were there? You saw this person?"

"Not exactly."

While Narda prowled about with a measuring tape, I related how the stowaway had vanished, and instead I'd run into Lenore and Agatha. "Old Mrs. Bryerly brought up her daughter's death in a fire, as if it were related."

"This was when?" Keith asked.

"Fifty years ago." More or less.

"Mrs. Bryerly suffers from dementia?"

"Yes to that, too."

"There you are." His shoulders lifted in dismissal.

Having seen bizarre information turn out to be key to a murder, I wasn't so quick to dismiss Lenore's memories. But neither could I figure out how events of half a century ago might shed light on Wes's murder.

I respected my detective buddy's down-to-earth pursuit of suspects and refusal to charge off after zebras. In medical lingo, a zebra is an exotic diagnosis, the type that medical students love to dig up, when a commonplace explanation is more likely.

On the other hand, zebras *do* exist.

"Keith? You gonna to stand there all night?" Narda gestured to him.

"Yes, dear. I mean, no, dear."

I joined in the hanging and positioning, primarily to safeguard my property. But I wasn't entirely displeased. This place could use a little fun, and neither of my housemates had been in the mood to entertain lately.

The thumping upstairs continued for half an hour, occasionally masked by our repositioning of furniture. Narda established a photo booth with a Parthenon backdrop, festooned doorways with fake grapes and adorned the dining room in royal purple and gold. In the entry, the cardboard god welcomed guests, his muscles flexed and his genitalia mercifully draped.

"How much did all this set you back?" I inquired of Keith.

"Don't ask." At close range, I noted circles beneath his eyes. These days, he was serving double duty at work and at home.

His phone rang. "Sparks," he barked, and listened. "No, sir. How the hell did they... I agree. We need to get ahead of this." It must be his sergeant or lieutenant, I thought. "No, we haven't released that to anyone outside the family. I haven't seen the website. A press conference? Yes, sir. I'll alert Mrs. Choate."

On my cell, I brought up *The Safe Harbor Journal*'s website. There it was: "Murder Weapon Traced to Tycoon's Son."

I showed it to Keith. Swearing, he tapped a number, presumably Cress's. As he talked to her, I scanned the story.

Byline: Soraya Montenegro. I'd encountered her before. Sophisticated and ambitious, she belonged to the get-a-scoop-at-any-cost school of journalism.

Citing unidentified sources, the story trumpeted the idea that Parker's knife might be the murder weapon in his brother-in-law's death. It also mentioned the text message sent from his phone that had lured Wes to the lot where his car was found.

The article ended with: "Police refused to explain why they haven't arrested Parker Bryerly. Could this be a case of unequal justice for the wealthy?"

I suspected that angle would be parroted by other reporters. If Cress's shop and Wes's studio weren't already flooded with media attention, they would be now.

On the cell, Keith was saying, "That's right, Mrs. Choate. You're welcome to attend or select someone to speak for you... I'm at his house right now. Yes, ma'am. I'll see you in a few minutes."

"Well?" I demanded when he clicked off.

"Cress Choate is at her parents' house and she intends to stop by here," he said.

"Why?"

"I'll let her explain."

Although not thrilled about yet another intrusion on my privacy, I sympathized with the young widow. Also, I was curious.

A few minutes later, I went to admit her. Or rather, them, since Tanya accompanied her friend.

A few days ago, I'd noted how strongly the women resembled each other. Not any more. Cress's cheekbones protruded and she'd skinned her hair back in a bun. By contrast, Tanya was blooming like a fertility goddess.

As they entered, the surrogate frowned at the gaudy mock statue. "Really?" Perhaps she disapproved of the levity, considering the circumstances, or she objected on artistic terms. Considering her high regard for my late wife, I suspected the latter.

"We're decorating for a friend's birthday party," I explained.

Narda introduced herself. Having been briefed on their identities, she paid her condolences to the widow before disappearing into the dining room.

Tory hurried downstairs, a blazer thrown over her exercise clothes. She shook hands with both guests, her manner restrained and professional. After all, the Bryerlys were clients.

As we took seats in the great room, Cress apologized for dropping in uninvited. "I was just around the corner. I meant to tell my parents the cause of death before they heard it on the news, but they'd already seen the website."

"Was your brother there?" Tory asked.

"No, he's at work. My parents keep saying I should expect him to be arrested. Like it's a foregone conclusion." Cress turned to Keith, who remained quietly observing. "You aren't going to charge Parker, are you? My brother didn't do it."

"Why do you believe that?" he asked.

"He's too honest. And gentle," Cress flared. "No matter how much he disliked Wes, he'd never attack him. Parker doesn't have a cruel bone in his body."

I tended to agreed. But no doubt Keith had heard similar claims about perpetrators who were stone-cold guilty.

"Someone's setting him up," Cress went on.

"Who?" Keith asked.

"I have no idea." She took a couple of short, fast breaths. "Gran told me about someone sneaking into Mr. Golden's van. The killer could be lurking around right now! Whoever's doing this must hate my family."

Interesting, that she viewed her husband's murder as an attack on the Bryerlys. To me, the motive seemed more likely to stem from some misstep—or worse—on Wes's part.

"Have you received threats, Mrs. Choate?" Keith asked.

"No."

"Have you encountered anything unusual—hang-up calls, puzzling emails, attempted identity theft?"

She didn't hesitate. "Not that I'm aware of. But since my husband died, I've had more important stuff on my mind."

"There are a million details to sort out," Tanya chimed in.

"And Mom's pestering me to find out what's in his exhibit, like I care!" Jumping up, Cress paced between the surrogate, Tory and me, her circuit limited by the photo booth on one side and Keith's stance on the other. "She's insisting we screen the pictures before Sunday. I don't think I can bear to do that."

"I'm willing to go to the gallery with your mother," Tanya offered. "Even though she treats me like a bad knock-off purse."

"You'd put up with her?" Cress paused near her friend. "That's so sweet. But I couldn't subject you to that."

While tensions between mothers and daughters are common, this animosity went far beyond that. My impressions of Bianca Bryerly put me squarely in Cress's corner.

"I don't mind," Tanya said. "I'll go." An exchange of glances appeared to settle the agreement.

Keith returned to his point. "Mrs. Choate, in light of this incident with Mr. Golden, I'm concerned about your safety, living alone. Perhaps you could stay with your parents for the present."

"Are you kidding? After someone sneaked in there and stole my brother's knife?" Cress said. "And now my parents act like they're ready to throw Parker under the bus. I'm afraid I'll lose my temper and tell them off."

"They engaged my services to try to clear your brother," Tory reminded her.

"Gran insisted they hire you, that's what." Her shoulders beginning to shake, Cress sank onto the couch.

Tanya hugged her. "It's okay. I'll stay with you."

"No offense, but you're hardly trained in security," Keith said.

"Cress has a burglar alarm," Tanya replied. "And she locks her doors, which is more than you can say for her parents."

"It's a good idea." Cress's breathing eased. "We'll have a pajama party. And I can keep an eye on her if she goes into labor."

"That's sensible." I'd been uneasy about Tanya being by herself so close to her due date. As for Cress needing protection, she could hardly hire armed guards to escort her everywhere, especially since there'd been no indication she was in the killer's sights.

The killer. Who the hell was doing this? I couldn't rule anyone out. Not even supposedly kind-hearted, geeky Parker.

Tory broke into my thoughts, addressing Cress. "I understand your grandparents died in a fire when your dad was a kid. What do you know about that?"

My interest pricked up. So did Keith's, I gathered as he slipped a notebook from his pocket.

"According to Gran, my grandmother Georgette ran off with my grandfather when she was seventeen," Cress said. "They never married, which I guess was a big deal back then."

"Back then" meant the Fifties. A very different era, indeed.

"They both drank and smoked," she continued. "Dad must have been five when their apartment caught fire. It was a miracle he escaped."

Keith paused in his scribbling. "Where did this occur?"

"New Orleans," she said. "Gran and Gramps lived in Texas and didn't find out for two years."

"Who took care of your father during that time?" Tory shifted in her chair.

"Foster parents," Cress said. "He doesn't like to discuss it."

Nothing I'd seen about millionaire software developer Noah Bryerly had mentioned a stint in foster care. The experience might have been traumatic. Still, despite Lenore's fixation on the past, I didn't see how it could be affecting current events.

"Oh!" Cress swung toward me. "I nearly forgot the whole reason I came here."

I raised an eyebrow.

"The police are holding a press conference tomorrow at 10 a.m. and I need someone to speak for me," she said. "Would you do it, please?"

I'd rather get my head shaved. Rather than say that, I

blurted, "What about your parents?"

"Seriously?" Cress shot back. "Mom's impossible and Dad hates publicity."

"I'll be there," Tory said.

"You should focus on protecting my brother, not me."

"How about a lawyer?" I hoped I didn't appear too much like a rat scurrying for cover, which was how I felt.

"He wouldn't know me like you do."

I was running out of alternatives. "Keith, what do you think?" Had my brain been clearer, I'd have reminded him that he owed me a favor, a big one, in view of the snowballing party plans. Such as insisting the police wouldn't allow a total amateur like me to participate.

Too late. "The wife's physician wouldn't be out of place at a news conference," he murmured.

But wait! I might have the perfect excuse. "Let me check my calendar." Thursday mornings were reserved for surgeries.

Bad luck: only two operations were scheduled, very early. Patients, like everyone else, tend to go on vacation in August.

I'd run out of excuses, and "I don't wanna" would sound childish. "I should be free by ten." I tried to suppress the "unfortunately" from my tone. "It won't last more than an hour, will it?"

"I damn well hope not," Keith said.

How did one speak for a widow at a news conference? "Should she prepare a statement for me to read?" I asked him.

"Not necessarily," he said. "You'll just be there to answer questions if she wants you to."

"I bet it'll stream live on that website. I'll follow along and call you if I need to," Cress said. "The bottom line is, if they ask about Parker, tell them my brother is one hundred percent innocent."

"Got it."

As we stood, Narda reappeared. "Hey, Cress and Tanya, it occurs to me that you guys could use a break. Why don't you come to my party Friday night? Mr. Golden is catering, and the food will be terrific. No need to bring a present."

"Thanks but I couldn't handle a party," Cress said. "Tanya, you should go."

Her friend wavered for a nanosecond. "I'd enjoy stopping by, if that's all right."

"Perfect." The black-haired nurse approached, hand extended. "May I?"

"Go ahead."

Narda rested her palm on Tanya's bulge. "Wow. I'm envious. You must be excited."

"I'm a surrogate, not the mom," Tanya said. "But it's amazing to think I'm carrying a little girl for my best friend. It's inspired me to think about having a baby for keeps someday."

"I can't wait to have kids, too." Narda beamed at Keith.

My friend looked trapped.

No more trapped than I felt, though. I didn't exactly wish to be called into an emergency surgery or suffer a dental abscess in the morning.

But I wouldn't have minded if I had.

CHAPTER ELEVEN

On television, news conferences always appeared to be simple affairs. Therefore, I didn't expect the level of preparation that went into Thursday morning's event.

By the time I arrived shortly past nine-thirty, the public information officer—a stocky fellow in his late thirties named Hank Driver—was busy setting up seats and equipment in front of the police department. The station occupies a two-story stucco building in Safe Harbor's Civic Center, adjacent to City Hall. On the upper plaza, there was space for a row of folding chairs and a table to hold recording gear. Steps led down to the lower level, where chairs had been arranged with a microphone stand in the center aisle.

The weather cut us a break. Despite a predicted afternoon high in the 90s, at this hour an ocean breeze kept the temperature comfortable.

News crews were arriving and reporters staking out seats. As I stood observing from the side, I recognized local reporter Soraya Montenegro, a dark-skinned young woman pretty enough to play a news reporter in a movie; a square-jawed Los Angeles commentator named Hayden O'Donnell, whom I'd seen on the six o'clock news; and Ian Martin, husband of the hospital's public relations director. Blue-eyed and gifted with movie-star looks, he hosted a video interview show and occasionally wrote stories for an international news syndicate.

The big guns had turned out.

Wasn't it common knowledge that the killer tends to insert himself into the proceedings? If so, he or she might be among the attendees, although no one struck me as suspicious. I assumed there was a plainclothes police presence, including a videographer capturing faces for later review.

Uneasily, I watched as more reporters, city officials, and a handful of others took seats. In the front row, Soraya spoke earnestly to a chubby man with longish hair over his ears. He rose and climbed the steps to adjust a videocam atop the table.

I placed him as Duncan Axelrod, the photographer Cress had hired to fulfill Wes's assignments. He must be continuing with other freelance work as well, in this case for *The Safe Harbor Journal.*

On my phone, I consulted the paper's website. A video showed Officer Driver talking in a low voice to a fifty-ish man in a crisply pressed uniform, although I couldn't hear their words. Cress had been on target about the live feed.

Keith emerged from the building, his tie knotted with rare precision. He gestured me to join him.

With the unpleasant sense of climbing a scaffold to my execution, I mounted the steps. I hoped the strong smell of antiseptic from my morning's surgeries wouldn't blow everyone away.

Keith introduced the older officer as Chief Jon Walters, who wore his blond hair cropped and his spine stiff. As we shook hands, his pale eyes assessed me coolly. Ex-military and not a man to cross, I thought.

More people gathered below. On my phone, I'd become a dot in the Journal's video pane.

I pressed Cress's number. "I'm watching you," she assured me. "Mom and Dad are with me."

"Glad you have support."

"If you can call it that."

After clicking off, I spotted Tory standing behind the lower-level seats. Wearing her gray-and-black business outfit, she studied each arrival.

At an upper-level microphone, Hank Driver welcomed everyone and introduced the policemen on the platform. "Also, Mrs. Choate has asked her physician, Dr. Eric Darcy, to represent her today."

I tried to appear calm and wise. Or at least to avoid giving the impression that rigor mortis had set in.

At the mic, Chief Walters recited the facts of Westlake Choate's murder. The car left at the harbor; the body found in the wetlands Tuesday morning, spotted by a jogger—I was grateful he once again avoided naming me—and the coroner's determination that cause of death was a stab wound.

"Didn't the murder weapon belong to the victim's brother-in-law, Parker Bryerly?" Soraya demanded. Kind of late to be asking that, I thought, since her newspaper had already claimed the knife was traced to him.

The murder weapon was under investigation, the chief said, tactfully dodging the question.

"Didn't Westlake Choate go to the harbor in response to a text message from Parker Bryerly?" Hayden O'Donnell boomed in the sonorous tones cultivated by TV newscasters.

"I'll let Detective Keith Sparks address your points. And I'd like to ask the press to use the microphone we've set up in the aisle there. This session is being recorded. Thank you." The chief stepped aside.

As Keith replaced his superior in front of the crowd, a woman with thick glasses and a protruding chin commandeered the lower mike. "Why haven't you arrested Parker Bryerly?"

"I must caution everyone not to jump to conclusions," Keith said. "All evidence is being carefully evaluated."

The woman hadn't finished. "Would you be this cautious if the suspect was poor and a minority?"

Irritation flashed across Keith's face but was quickly subdued. To the obvious frustration of the questioner, he produced another bland statement about the need for thoroughness.

Questions flew. Had yesterday's "attack" (the reporter's word) on the Golden Fine Foods caterer been related to the murder? That remained to be determined, Keith said.

Was Westlake Choate drugged before his murder? Toxicology tests were pending. But hadn't a bottle of flavored water containing a sedative been found at the murder scene?

It was the first I'd heard of a possible drugging, and I wished my friend would answer. But he once again declined to reveal details of an ongoing investigation.

The press had done its homework. I wondered how they'd ferreted out their information. So, most likely, did Keith.

The questions continued. How had the victim been transported from the harbor to the wetlands? Had he walked or ridden with someone? Did that indicate he'd known his killer?

Everything was under investigation.

What about reports that the victim had been beaten as well as drugged and stabbed? He'd had injuries consistent with defending himself in a struggle, Keith responded, but declined to describe them.

Was there something about the injuries he wanted to keep from the public? I wondered. He'd told me that police often withheld information that might later prove important in identifying the culprit.

Ian Martin took the lower mic. "According to the victim's Facebook page, he and his wife had commissioned a surrogate who's now pregnant with their baby. Could that have been a factor in his murder?"

"In what way?" Keith asked.

"My question is for Dr. Darcy."

Oh, hell.

Stiffly, I uncoiled and joined Keith. "I'm not aware of any disputes affecting the surrogacy," I said.

"Isn't it unusual to go outside the hospital's surrogacy program?" Ian held onto the mic. Behind him, Hayden and Soraya were angling to grab it the moment he let go.

"Not really." I stopped there. As a doctor, I'm in the habit of explaining things at length. In this situation, however, I considered the details private, even though Cress had urged me to represent her.

"The surrogate worked for both Mr. and Mrs. Choate in their businesses," Ian said. "Isn't serving as their surrogate a conflict of interest?"

I resented the implication that Tanya had been coerced or had some selfish motive. Acting defensive, however, was likely to backfire. "I don't assist with a surrogacy unless all parties sign a contract that safeguards their interests."

When Ian relinquished the mic, Hayden seized it. "Does Mrs. Choate believe her brother killed her husband?" I could have sworn he bared wolfish teeth, as if he'd slashed a deer's throat and was closing in for the kill.

"Absolutely not." What a relief to be able to speak firmly. "Mrs. Choate has complete confidence in Parker Bryerly's innocence."

He accepted this, if not happily. I dared to imagine the worst was over.

It was Soraya's turn. "My source claims Westlake Choate was having an affair. Can either of you confirm that? Was that why someone murdered him?"

Even though we were outdoors, the space around me felt suddenly airless. Beneath the surface, I'd had the same nagging concern.

Keith moved in again. "We have no information on that."

I took the opportunity to resume my seat. No reason to deal with wild speculation, or risk displaying my doubts.

Half a dozen reporters leaped up, piling questions one on top of the other. Who was the victim's lover? Had his wife discovered the affair?

"We have no information," Keith repeated. "Thank you for joining us."

The news conference was over. I felt as if I'd just performed a twelve-hour operation where the patient had nearly died twice. And remained unstable.

Now I had to talk to Cress.

She answered immediately. "That isn't true about Wes cheating! You should have told them, Dr Darcy. My husband wouldn't do that!"

"Whatever I said would only have inflamed them." Especially if they'd picked up on my hesitation. "The media feeds on scandal. It's cruel that it comes at your expense. Let's hope it blows over quickly."

"I can't stand it! I should hold my own press conference and issue a public denial."

Worst idea ever. "Cress, they'll twist it against you." I had to divert her from such a suicidal course. "Focus on honoring your husband's memory. What about your mother's request to preview the exhibit? The two of you could visit the gallery together."

"Tanya's doing that for me," she said.

Leaving Cress alone to dwell on her rage at the media? I shivered to imagine what she might post online. "You're his wife. You can ensure the pictures are displayed properly."

She might also benefit from a bit of mother-daughter bonding, if that were possible. Considering my positive impressions of both Parker and Cress, surely a mothering instinct lurked somewhere inside Bianca Bryerly.

"I've been curious about the photos," she conceded. "And I suppose I owe him that. I'll consider it."

After she ended the call, I pressed Tanya's number. If she'd watched the conference, her blood pressure might be spiking.

However, she told me she'd been too busy at the studio. The publicity about Wes's murder had, to her surprise, brought in new clients. "I'm keeping them occupied until Duncan gets here from the police station."

She was aware of the photographer's work for the news site. Good. The fewer secrets, the better.

As for how she would react when she heard the press accusations of an affair, I hoped she'd be as outraged as Cress. And that my suspicions about her were wrong.

As I headed for the parking lot, Tory fell into step. "What a pack of hyenas," she said. "I'm beginning to wonder if Dad's stowaway was a reporter trying to eavesdrop on his phone conversations or snag an interview."

"Until he freaked out and nearly crashed the van," I noted.

"Yeah. If I find out who it was, I'll..." Her fists balled.

"Punch them out?"

She grimaced. "Have them brought up on charges."

We paused by my car. "No suspects in attendance?" I asked.

"I suspect everyone."

That was unhelpful. "Dig up anything more about Wes?"

My sister-in-law shrugged. "Witnesses from Sunday night's wedding described him as being in high spirits early on. Then his mood darkened. No obvious reason."

"The I-know-what-you-did text from Parker's phone?" I suggested.

"That's my bet." With a wave, she left.

That was my bet, too. Wes Choate had been hiding something.

I wished I knew what.

CHAPTER TWELVE

At the hospital that morning, no doubt patients had been examined, ultrasounds provided, and other normal business conducted. Yet when I arrived to check on Maggie Majors's condition, a murmur trailed me through the halls.

Had the entire staff been glued to the news conference? And not only the staff, I discovered. Patients, too.

"You're famous, Dr. Darcy," the surrogate told me cheerily from her bed. "Photogenic, too. It's those classic features."

"Thanks." I got right down to business. "Any more labor pains?" Her chart indicated contractions had stopped, but patient perceptions are important.

"All gone."

The baby's heartbeat remained normal, as did the mother's blood pressure. "Let's keep you here another day. If everything's fine, you can resume bed rest at home."

"I'd like that. So would my family." That included her husband, their eight-year-old daughter, and a teenage stepson.

Her screening by the surrogacy program had included assessing her family's attitudes. Maggie had told me earlier that the children were supportive of her bearing a baby for a childless couple. Nevertheless, being hospitalized and away from them must be inconvenient.

"Anything else on your mind?" Patients often have to be encouraged to mention what's bothering them.

"I'm glad I'm not the surrogate for the Choate couple," Maggie said. "What an awful situation."

"Tragic," I agreed. After making sure no other matters were troubling her, I took my leave.

Since I had no patients scheduled for an hour, I went to the cafeteria. The price of lunch, unfortunately, included running a gauntlet of stares. Nor was I thrilled, as I paid the cashier, to realize it was too hot to retreat to the semi-secluded patio.

Tray in hand, I surveyed the bustling room. Doctors, nurses, receptionists and technicians regarded me with more than ordinary interest. I was considering transferring my food to a carry-out carton when a paisley-printed surgical cap bobbed into place beside me.

"I used to assume police investigations were exciting," said Rod Vintner, the anesthesiologist who shared his house with Keely as well as his wife and daughters. "My girls videoed them walking a grid pattern in the wetlands. It's painstaking and frustrating, kind of like doing brain surgery on a politician. You hope you'll find something worthwhile in there, but what are the odds?"

"Any place we can eat in peace?" I asked.

He jerked his bearded chin toward a table where Jeremiah sat alone. Not that other doctors shun our weird colleague; it's simply that he's more comfortable by himself. If he spots me already in place, however, he joins me. Until today, I'd never deliberately joined him.

"I thought you weren't crazy about Dr. Schwartz," I said.

"He's grown on me." When Rod set out in that direction, I accompanied him.

En route, I asked, "Did you hear anything from the wetlands

Monday morning? Besides coyotes, I mean." With Wes fighting his attacker, there should have been some noise.

"The police already asked, but I'm afraid we're a loud bunch," Rod said. "We were probably yakking our heads off over breakfast. Plus the crime scene's quite a distance from the house."

As we rested our trays, Jeremiah's penetrating gaze drilled into me. "You are now the center of attention," he informed me. "Is it pleasant?"

"It sucks," I said.

"I am not surprised," he responded. "The press is unreasonable and impulsive. They do not appear to seek the truth."

"Journalism students who're overly concerned with the truth get booted out," Rod cracked.

"How can one be overly concerned with the truth?" Jeremiah asked.

"It requires standing up to your professors," Rod answered. "They hate that."

I returned to Jeremiah's topic. "If you were a reporter, what questions would you ask?"

"I would ask who else had access to Parker Bryerly's phone and knife," he said.

"Quite a few people." None of whom I could imagine murdering Wes and framing Parker. "Plus the Bryerlys leave their side door unlocked when they're home. Someone else might have sneaked in."

"Now we enter the realm of the super-genius arch criminal beloved of bad writers," Rod scoffed. "He can slip into a house unseen at precisely the opportune moment, conduct his nefarious business, and remove himself without leaving a shred of evidence."

He'd touched on a matter that bothered me. While I

couldn't picture any of the attendees at Sunday night's dinner as the killer, there'd been no way for an outsider to know that Parker had left his phone in the bathroom. It simply wasn't credible that an outsider had sent a text unobserved, not to mention swiping the knife from where Morris had left it.

"Then there is the matter of the surrogacy," Jeremiah said. "A reporter introduced this element because he believes it to be sensational, as if sex were involved, which it is not."

"Oh, come on, Jeremiah," Rod countered. "Can't the press have a little fun?"

"It is not their job to have fun at the expense of our patients," my colleague said.

I agreed with him on that.

When I reached my office, Farrah handed me the sheets she'd printed out on the next group of patients. She started to speak, cleared her throat, and turned away.

"Hey, what was that about?" I asked.

"I'm sorry?" She swung back.

"You were about to say something."

The nurse smiled. "Just that you look fantastic on video. Have you considered hosting a series on YouTube? Talking to women about medical issues."

"I prefer practicing medicine in person," I said. "But thank you."

"You'd be a hit," she replied. "Well, this way we get to keep you to ourselves."

"Exactly." It was flattering, having a nurse who thought well of me. I regretted that I was occasionally late and sometimes snappish. But I had no doubt I'd do it again.

For the rest of the day, I put the situation out of my head. It was growing late when Farrah informed me that Tanya Nichols had arrived without an appointment.

"That's fine." I do my best to be flexible, especially with

pregnant patients. If you require predictable hours, obstetrics is the wrong specialty for you.

While Farrah prepped her, I caught up on my email. In addition to the usual patient inquiries, medical updates and hospital business, there were several media requests for interviews. I deleted them.

In the exam room, Tanya greeted me with a subdued air. Her rounded cheeks made her appear especially young, reminding me of the girl who used to tag along after her big sister Shana and my wife, both six years her elder. Despite her artistic talent, Tanya had lacked their focus, taking a few community college art classes rather than pursuing a degree. But her upbeat personality had endeared her to everyone.

Noting the worried pucker between her eyebrows, I asked what was wrong.

"I'm having contractions," she said. "I think they're just Braxton Hicks, so I didn't disturb Cress. She's got enough to deal with already."

"Is she okay?"

"She's gone to stay with her parents. A couple of reporters showed up at the studio and the shop. Living upstairs, she feels too vulnerable."

"Understandable," I said. "Tell me what you're experiencing."

"Tightening in the abdomen. It comes and goes."

"Does it hurt?"

"Not really."

That fit her self-diagnosis of Braxton Hicks, mild contractions also known as false labor. They're believed to be nature's way of preparing the body for childbirth.

Were they getting stronger? No. Lasting longer? Tanya responded in the negative.

"Are you feeling them now?"

"They've stopped."

An exam showed no cervical changes to indicate true labor had begun. When I informed her of this, she nodded tensely.

Something must be weighing on her mind. "What's bothering you?"

"It's, uh…" She halted.

Time for the doctor to play detective, I thought, and took a stab at it. "Did you have a chance to watch the press conference?"

"Yeah." Another pause.

At the end of a long day, I had to dig deep for patience. "Did it upset you that a reporter asked about the surrogacy?"

"Not that."

I fought to keep my tone even. "What, then?"

Tanya swallowed. "Why did they bring up that stuff about Wes having an affair?"

Touchy issue. I went on high alert. "People spread rumors."

"About me?"

"Not specifically." I wasn't sure I wanted to hear more, but listening was part of my job. And, as Lenore had said, I'd helped put Tanya in the middle of things.

"Well, it happened." She toyed with a strand of hair. "I wish, wish, wish it hadn't."

So do I. "What happened?"

The story spilled out. "Wes was shooting pictures of me one night to document the pregnancy, and I let him talk me into removing the bikini. He claimed the images would be more honest, that I should be proud of my body. And that he'd never show them to anyone."

I glanced toward the door, confirming that it was shut. This was not a revelation for my staff to overhear. "Go on."

"He kept adjusting the lighting and touching me." Tanya shivered. "My skin was hypersensitive. Anyway, we did it.

There in the studio, on the couch. Physically, it felt amazing. But afterwards I was so, so sorry."

I held onto my temper. The guy might be dead, but that didn't excuse his betrayal of his wife or his taking advantage—from my perspective—of their vulnerable surrogate. "How did Wes behave afterwards?"

"He tried to get me alone again but I avoided him." Tears dampened her lashes. "How could they know? The press, I mean."

"They don't. They're fishing."

"Cress hasn't seen the nude pictures. What if he put them in the exhibit? What if she sees them and figures it out?" Tanya rubbed her fingers together as if trying to peel off a residue of rubber cement.

"Let's not borrow trouble," I said. "Wes might have kept his word about not showing them to anyone." Surely the bastard had had that much decency. Well, not surely. Maybe.

"Cress decided to preview the exhibit tomorrow with her mother." Tanya reached down as if to hug her knees. Blocked by her large abdomen, she settled for stretching.

"You must be uncomfortable. Let's get you down." I assisted her from the table.

Easing onto her feet, Tanya said, "If Cress finds out, she'll hate me forever."

I couldn't deny that, and I didn't try. "I'm concerned about the stress this is putting on you. I'd like you to talk to our staff psychologist."

"No!"

It was her choice. Moving on, I asked, "Has this affected your attitude toward the pregnancy?"

She thought it over. "I hate Wes for what he did to me and Cress. I still love little Georgie, though. I'm glad to be giving her life."

"That's good." I'd seen only minimal risk in agreeing to participate in a surrogacy outside the hospital's program. It violated no ethical or legal rules, and had seemed a blessing for all concerned. Until now.

"When you told me most surrogates use eggs from a third party, I didn't think it mattered," Tanya went on. "Just the opposite. I liked that Cress would have a baby that came from me."

That reminded me: she wasn't just carrying a baby for Cress and Wes. The child had been conceived with her egg, her genetic heritage. "What do you think about that now?"

"I keep remembering something Lydia told me."

How unexpected for my wife's name to crop up. "What did she say?"

"That you grow up thinking your ancestors were merely links in a chain that led to you," she said. "But when you're ready to have kids, you discover you're part of a long line that stretches into the future."

How beautiful, and puzzling. "That's strange, since Lydia didn't want children."

Tanya frowned. "Of course she did. My gosh, Eric, how could you not know that?"

"Because..." Because I'd believed that was the reason she left me. "She got upset when I brought up having children."

One night after delivering a half-dozen babies and losing my heart to each of them, I'd collapsed at home and told Lydia how much I longed to be a father. I'd acknowledged that she was still struggling to establish herself as an artist, that I respected her need for private time and treasured our closeness as a couple. But someday, I'd said, while we were still young enough...

From that night on, she'd changed, confiding in me less, coming and going without explanation, crying when she didn't think I'd notice. She'd refused to discuss her moods and, when I suggested marriage counseling, Lydia had insisted on working this out by herself.

It had seemed obvious to me that she'd felt pressured into motherhood. In all our years together, we'd never specifically discussed the subject. There'd been casual references to having kids someday and she hadn't rejected the idea, but neither had she endorsed it.

I'd assumed that, eventually, she would trust me enough to open up. Instead, she'd written a new will asking to be buried in Israel should she die there, and gone on a journey to learn what had happened to her grandparents. Her mother had quoted her father as telling conflicting stories: that after the Holocaust, they'd found each other again and reached Israel, then disappeared; that they'd been so overwhelmed by survivor's guilt that they'd committed suicide; that they'd been murdered.

Avram Silver and an older brother or cousin—Lydia's mother hadn't been sure which—had grown up in a kibbutz. They'd lost touch after Avram emigrated to the U.S. as a young man, and he'd expressed no interest in making contact with relatives in Israel.

Lydia had assured me she was in no danger from her compulsion to find the truth. Yet she'd fallen or jumped to her death as she toured the mountain fortress of Masada, the site where, in 73 A.D., almost a thousand Jewish men, women and children had died by their choice rather than be enslaved by the Romans.

The authorities had ruled my wife's death an accidental fall due to intense heat. Tory, who'd flown to Israel, had confirmed that such a thing was possible. Temperatures had exceeded 100 degrees that day and the perimeter wasn't well secured. Neither she nor I could be sure of the truth.

One thing Tory did learn from Lydia's tour guide: prior to visiting Masada, my wife had arranged to meet someone in Jerusalem. There'd been no email or phone records indicating who it was. Perhaps it had been a fellow artist, a gallery owner who might show her work, or someone with information about her family. But always, in my mind, the events leading to her death had stemmed from the night I revealed how strongly I yearned for children.

"I'm surprised to hear she reacted that way." Tanya's voice snapped me out of my thoughts. "I wonder what she did with the picture."

"Which picture?" Lydia had left many artworks. None involved children, that I could recall.

"This fantasy piece with kids and a castle," she said. "I don't believe she'd have sold it. She loved it."

"It doesn't sound familiar." However, after Lydia's death, I'd been too grief-stricken to go through her possessions. I'd asked my sister-in-law to donate the clothes, personal items and art supplies, and store the creative pieces in the attic. "I'll look for it. Thanks."

"Glad to help."

I retrained my attention on my patient. "By the way, if Cress is at her parents' house, where are you staying?"

"I'm back at my apartment," Tanya said. "The reporters haven't found it, thank goodness."

Still, I wasn't pleased that no one was watching over her. "I'm concerned that you're alone. Is there anyone who can stay with you?"

Tanya smiled. "Duncan lives in the same complex. He promised to bring dinner tonight."

I recalled the chunky fellow who'd adjusted the videocam at the conference. "Good. You should eat regular meals." *And have a protector, if that's what he is.*

"Yes, Dr. Mommy," she teased.

We took our leave. Since she was the last patient of the day, I went home and, torn between fear and eagerness, climbed the stairs to the attic.

Daylight filtering through narrow windows illuminated the modest third story, which covered less than half of the house's footprint. In the main chamber, tarps protected a scattering of furniture, suitcases, boxes, and a file cabinet of old medical records. A second, slope-roofed room had served as Lydia's studio while my father was alive. Emptied out when she took over the downstairs conservatory, it had become a storage space for her art.

I reviewed the works, stored upright beneath dust cloths. Combining fabric, paints and objects, they featured impressionistic landscapes, strange forests glowing with eyes, and indistinct female figures. The colors shaded from rainbow pastels to grayish-purples. None included children.

Then I lifted a dust cloth to reveal a picture I'd never seen before. Roughly three feet high by two feet wide, it had been created with mixed media. As was her custom, Lydia had affixed and layered objects, including bits of cloth and photographs, painting over and around them to integrate her concept.

Bright colors, more intense than the hues she usually chose, brought a storybook scene to life. From a castle balcony leaned a woman with hair cascading to the ground. It appeared to be real hair, stiff with gold paint. Between the tresses, children peeked out, while others darted across the castle grounds, rolling hoops and chasing a unicorn. It had fewer of the subtle textures and dark tones that characterized her other works.

I checked the back of the frame. A white sticker bore a date six months before her death, along with a few words hand-lettered in Hebrew. Aside from knowing that the language reads from right to left, I was out of my league.

On my phone, I snapped a picture and pasted it into a translation app. In English, it read: "My Dream, Our Family."

My stomach tightened. How could Lydia have poured her warmth and lightness and longing into this painting without sharing it? Yet the word "our" implied both of us.

If my desire for fatherhood hadn't pushed my wife away, what had? Why had she become secretive in her last months?

No answers occurred to me as I stared through a window into the night. On the hill above, a light flicked on at the Bryerly house. Around the deceptively transparent glass structure, shadows lengthened.

Cress was there, sheltering with her family. Living among secrets, as I had been without knowing it.

Since I couldn't resolve the questions about my life, I focused on my neighbors. Had Parker Bryerly's family protected him in his great-grandfather's drowning death and were they closing ranks around him again? What about his great-grandmother's tale of a fire half a century ago and a child—Cress and Parker's father, Noah—missing for two years in foster care?

I couldn't grasp what connection Wes might have to any of this. One fact in particular troubled me: As long as Wes's murderer and the motive remained unidentified, there was no telling who else might be at risk.

CHAPTER THIRTEEN

Despite my nagging sense of danger, Friday passed quietly. At the hospital, seeing no further signs of imminent birth or complications, I released a cheerful Maggie to the care of her husband.

Calls from the press dropped off. A controversial pop star had tweeted a picture of herself in a thong bikini; a drunken quarterback defecated on his neighbor's lawn; and a politician up for reelection was videoed kicking his dog. The four-day-old murder dropped from sight.

By phone, Tanya assured me she was fine and that Duncan was keeping an eye on her. Also, she reported, Wes's body had been turned over to the funeral home and a small, private service was scheduled for Saturday, followed by a gathering at the Bryerly house.

"I hate funerals but I should go," she said. "To support Cress."

"Good for you." Funerals depress me. Since the event was private and the family hadn't contacted me, I presumed I could tactfully stay home.

As she signed off, Tanya confirmed her decision to stop by Narda's party later. With everything that had happened, I'd almost forgotten I could look forward to loud music and a bunch of strangers invading my house.

I wondered if Keith had followed my advice about buying jewelry for the birthday girl. Too bad he didn't enjoy selecting and giving gifts. For me, it had been a joy to see Lydia's face light up when I presented her with a messenger bag designed to carry her art supplies, or brought flowers in her favorite colors.

When I arrived home, the scents of cheese and spices drifted to me. Chef hat and white coat in place, Morris bustled about the kitchen, preparing food for the party. In the dining room, his assistant, Helen, was setting out punch, soft drinks and snacks.

Beneath the cooking aromas lingered a touch of lemon cleanser. En route to the stairs, I bumped into Keely storing the vacuum cleaner in the hall closet.

"Excellent job," I told my housekeeper.

She grunted. "It'll be a mess tomorrow."

"Narda promised to straighten up," I reminded her.

"That one? Don't count on it." Keely arched her shoulders, from which issued a loud crack. Apparently this didn't hurt, because she continued in the same nasal tone, "I've got a bad feeling about this."

"I promise to stand guard over the family silver," I joked. The guest list Narda had emailed included about thirty people, mostly her colleagues from Heights View Medical Center. Hardly my idea of wild party animals. The worst damage was likely to be spilled food.

"Mark my words, this won't end well," Keely intoned. "There's no stopping fate." After uttering that pronouncement more suited to a Greek tragedy than a Greek funfest, she departed.

Curious as to how my sister-in-law was handling the

situation, I proceeded to the conservatory. From the tall mullioned windows, backlight cast a reddish-brown halo around Tory's head where she sat at her chipped desk.

"Oh, it's you," came the greeting.

I noted her faded jeans and T-shirt. "Not in a party mood, I see."

"Too busy doing my job." She tapped a key on the computer.

"Anything new?"

"Odds and ends." Tilting her chair back, Tory steepled her fingers. "Agatha Kozma was sponsored into the U.S. by Bianca Bryerly half a dozen years ago to be Lenore Bryerly's caretaker. Supposedly Agatha's an old friend, although I don't know how an Italian-American became friends with a woman from Greece."

"Parker said his parents took a memorable trip there many years ago. Maybe she was a tour guide." Some of my well-traveled colleagues stay in touch with guides for years.

Tory shrugged.

"Learn anything about Bianca?" Cress's mother intrigued me, perhaps because she was full of contradictions—stylish, tightly wound, not especially maternal yet willing to accompany her daughter to preview Wes's photos. And, obviously, she'd been kind to Agatha.

"Her maiden name was Bianca Fortuna. She grew up in Florida, where she won a few beauty contests."

That, I could picture. But... "Why does she have an accent if she grew up in Florida?"

"Maybe her parents spoke Italian at home," Tory said. "They're deceased, by the way. Oh, and here's a funny note: at the pageants, her talent was a presentation on the dangers of smoking."

How ironic. "Wonder when she got addicted."

"She moved to San Francisco to work as a secretary, which is how she met her husband," Tory said. "Maybe he smoked, although that was especially foolish in his case."

"Why's that?"

"The fire that killed his parents in New Orleans may have been caused by smoking," she explained. "I couldn't find much about it, though. Hurricane Katrina wiped out a lot of records."

"Interesting that you're digging into your clients' pasts," I noted. "You could just ask the Bryerlys about this stuff."

"People lie or get their facts muddled," Tory said. "In case Parker's prosecuted, it's my job to prepare his attorney for any dirt the district attorney might dig up."

That made sense. "What about Saul's death?"

She tapped her fingers together. "Official cause of death was drowning in salt water. He had bruising consistent with falling overboard and getting smacked by the boat. Nothing suspicious except that a ninety-year-old has to be insane or senile to go sailing alone."

I hadn't forgotten Lenore's hint. "If he was alone."

"No indication of a second person on board." Tory pushed away from the desk. "Now I'll amscray before the barbarian hordes descend."

"You're leaving?" I felt abandoned.

"Going to the movies." Rising, she shooed me toward the hall.

"Alone?"

"Believe it or not, I have friends." She locked the office behind us and headed for the garage. "Enjoy yourself."

"I plan to." At a minimum, I expected to eat well.

By seven o'clock, a subdued Keith had arrived with Narda, who vibrated as if preparing for liftoff. Shimmering in a golden off-the-shoulder dress, she sped through the house, tasting snacks, activating the music (the theme from *Zorba the Greek*, for starters) and sampling a glass of ouzo, an anise-flavored liqueur that I'd tried and crossed off my list.

"You'd think it was Christmas," Keith observed, watching Morris remove pastries from the oven. "My gift better not disappoint her."

"Jewelry?" I inquired.

He nodded. "Cost five hundred bucks, on sale. Worth twice as much."

"Isn't it the thought that counts?"

"In your dreams."

Half an hour later, a concerto of doorbell rings ushered in guests. Narda welcomed them all and introduced those I didn't know. I politely repeated and promptly forgot their names.

Gifts piled up on the dining room sideboard. Shoes were kicked off, dancing occurred, and food vanished along with beverages. No drunken behavior claimed my attention, nor, as far as I could tell, Keith's.

I wondered whether he'd arrest his girlfriend's party guests for DUIs. Probably confiscate their keys before they got behind the wheel. Plus, these being hospital staffers experienced in the carnage of emergency rooms, they should have arranged designated drivers.

I didn't notice Tanya's arrival until she appeared amid a cluster of women, several of whom patted her abdomen. Judging by the chatter, they shared Narda's enthusiasm for babies. If Tanya went into labor tonight, she'd be surrounded by expert and enthusiastic nurses.

After about an hour, Helen took her leave, having set out the last of the refreshments. My father-in-law cleaned the kitchen and retreated to his quarters.

A few others left, too, summoned to the hospital or citing shift schedules. When about twenty of her friends remained, a giddy Narda gathered them in the dining room to witness the opening of the gifts.

"It's like a children's party," Tanya told me. "How sweet."

I scooted over a chair for her. "Relax." Standing while pregnant puts a strain on a woman's lower back and can cause blood pressure to drop.

"Thanks, Eric." She sank down.

At the sideboard, Narda tore into the wrappings, casting them to the floor. Her friends cheered each item: a charm bracelet, gift cards for gourmet coffee and chocolates, a rhinestone-trimmed phone case, wine glasses etched with "I deserve this." Tanya had bought a mug with a flattering motto about nurses.

Narda was clearly saving a small box for last. When Keith drifted up beside me, he muttered, "There it is."

"Good luck."

Narda plowed through the last of the pile with mounting eagerness. What was she expecting? Surely not an engagement ring. Keith would never propose in front of all these people. I doubted he'd propose under any circumstances.

The moment arrived. Beaming, the birthday girl pried the glossy paper and bow from the small box. Several women leaned forward.

From inside, Narda lifted a gold necklace. Even in the dim light, its diamond-accented centerpiece glittered. Oohs and ahs issued from onlookers.

"It's a Greek key design," Keith told me under his breath.

"That's lovely," Tanya said.

Narda's expression shifted from disbelief to dismay. Evidently this was not what she'd been hoping for.

"Oh, sh... damn," Keith growled, perhaps tempering his language for Tanya's sake. "What's she in a snit about this time?"

The nurse glared at him. "I didn't want a key necklace, I

wanted the key to your apartment! Can't you take a hint?"

My friend's mouth tightened. To his credit, he didn't answer with the truth, that the main purpose of holding Narda's party at my home instead of his had been to prevent her from establishing a beachhead.

I braced to catch the necklace if she threw it at him. Instead, she stalked out of the room. A moment later, the front door slammed.

"She's drunk," Tanya said.

"Not that drunk. She took the necklace." Keith showed no sign of pursuing his girlfriend. "You know what? I don't care."

With half-hearted thanks and a general air of embarrassment, the sheepish guests began to disperse, leaving a mess.

"Hold on." I fetched trash bags from the kitchen and handed them around. "Narda will appreciate not having to return tomorrow to clean." That was putting it delicately, since I doubted she meant to.

Most of the partygoers pitched in gamely. They carted out debris, wiped surfaces and stored food and beverages. A couple of the women hung around long enough to sweep and vacuum. Good people, I thought as I thanked them.

I provided a shopping bag for them to cart off Narda's remaining gifts for her. Grinning, one lady accepted the nearly naked mock statue.

Despite Keely's dire prophecy, the only real damage had been to Keith's pride. And his wallet. "If that's the worst thing the fates have in store tonight, it's not too bad," I said, and then wished I hadn't. Seemed like bad luck.

"Okay if I take a few leftovers for Duncan?" Tanya asked.

"Help yourself."

I was sealing a container for her when the doorbell rang. Assuming Narda had returned, I went to answer.

But it wasn't Narda. It was someone even angrier, and far more vengeful.

CHAPTER FOURTEEN

"Where the hell is she?" Like a Fury from mythology, Cress stalked into the front hall. Tangled brown hair fanned around her face, and weeping had left red marks on her cheeks. "I know she's here. Her car's parked down the block."

Obviously, she referred to Tanya. "Tell me what's wrong," I said soothingly.

A wasted effort. "You'll find out soon enough." She barreled past me.

This afternoon, I recalled, Cress and her mother had planned to preview Wes's exhibit. Oh, hell. Had he included nude pictures of the surrogate?

If so, his wife must have drawn the obvious conclusion. From her parents' house above mine, she could have spotted Tanya's car and waited, seething, until my guests left.

In the great room, she halted, quivering with anger. Behind the kitchen counter, Tanya stood stock-still. Neither woman paid any attention to Keith, who was observing the scene with a homicide detective's interest.

"You and Wes were having an affair," Cress snarled.

"Why do you think that?" Tanya asked. A last-ditch effort to stave off disaster.

"He photographed you naked, and you never told me. I guess I was supposed to find out when he put them in his exhibit for the whole world to see."

Keith's jaw tightened at this revelation. Apparently when Trent Horner visited the gallery, he'd missed the implication of an affair with the surrogate.

"I can't believe he did that." Tanya dropped any attempt to protest. "How many? How bad are they?"

"Just one. Shot from behind, but I recognized your fat butt," the outraged widow cried. "My Mom did, too, after I pointed it out. You were his whore. Don't lie to me!"

Breathing hard, Cress took a step forward. Keith and I tensed, ready to intervene if she attacked.

"I'm sorry," Tanya said.

"That's it? You're sorry?" Cress flung at her. "You've been carrying his child and laughing at me!"

"It isn't like that." Tanya clutched the edge of the counter. "Wes talked me into posing for those photos and we got carried away. It was wrong. I feel awful. It only happened once."

"That's your excuse, you cheap trash?" Cress didn't seem to notice sparkles drifting across her from an overhead decoration. "I only agreed to use you as our surrogate because Wes wanted to save money. But he had his grubby hands on you already, didn't he? I bet you didn't bother to wait for the insemination."

"That's not true!" Tanya blinked against tears. "I did this for you."

"A great big favor, is that it?" Cress sneered. "Well, you can stuff it!"

Tanya stared at her friend. "You don't mean that."

"I want nothing to do with the baby my husband planted inside you."

I wished I knew how to stop this runaway train. Nothing

occurred to me.

"Fine," Tanya retorted. "I'll do that."

"Do what?"

"Keep Georgie."

Oh, crap.

The implications of their quarrel finally seemed to dawn on Cress. "You can't! You signed a contract."

"Which you just washed your hands of," was the furious response. "I've got witnesses. Don't I, Dr. Darcy?"

I refused to be dragged into this. "You both need to cool down. Cress has had a shock and so have you."

"You heard her! She didn't want me as the surrogate." Tanya shut the lid on a plastic storage tub. "And she rejected the baby."

"You're turning my words against me." After a moment's hesitation, Cress reclaimed her rage. "You manipulative little bitch!"

I raised my hands. "You've both said too much. Let's not make it worse."

"I can't tell you how much I regret sleeping with Wes," Tanya said. "But it had nothing to do with my pregnancy. Or this innocent baby."

"Who happens to be your love child!" Cress flung at her. "Every time I look at her, I'll see my husband's betrayal."

"You're irrational."

"And you're a slut!"

They might have been back in high school. But they weren't, and a child's future was on the line.

"I won't let you punish my daughter," the surrogate said tightly. "She deserves a real mother."

"You'll be hearing from my lawyer." With that parting thrust, Cress spun around.

After her former friend departed, Tanya poured herself a

glass of milk. Her hand shook.

Keely had been right about this evening, I thought. A disaster on all fronts.

The least perturbed person in the house retrieved a beer from the fridge. "What time's Tory getting home?" Keith asked.

That was his reaction? "She went to the movies with friends."

"Which friends?"

"She didn't specify."

Tanya settled at the table with her milk. I squelched an urge to comfort her. Having cheated with her best friend's husband, she could hardly expect absolution. Nor could I offer encouragement regarding the legalities, since I suspected a judge would assign custody to Cress. Words spoken in anger are no match for a signed, witnessed contract.

As for the baby's future, I believed that, once the initial shock and rage abated, Cress's maternal instincts would return. If not, she had no business keeping the child.

What a mess.

Lenore had accused me of contributing to her great-granddaughter's unhappiness and of putting Tanya in the middle. Perceptive old lady, despite her mental deficits.

"Guess I won't be attending the funeral tomorrow. Or the exhibit Sunday." Tanya shuddered. "And I'll have to find a new birthing partner."

"The nurses will help you," I said. "But are you in a position to raise a child alone?"

She stroked her abdomen. "Maybe not, but I have to protect Georgie. What if Cress hates her because she's mine and Wes's?"

Cress had essentially said as much, in the heat of battle. "Don't rush into a decision. I strongly recommend counseling for you both."

"Maybe. I can't think about it tonight." Tanya carried her glass to the sink. "I'm heading home."

It was after eleven. "I'll walk you to your car."

She waved away the offer. "I haven't turned into some wimp who has to lean on a guy. Even you, Eric. It's not as if there are gangs roaming your neighborhood."

Despite my protective instinct, I decided not to argue. "Keep your phone handy."

"I always have my phone handy." At the front door, Tanya paused. "Eric?"

"Yes?" I hoped she'd changed her mind about walking by herself.

"Do you think my ass is fat?"

That was what worried her? "I think you're a healthy pregnant woman."

Her mouth curved. "I'll take that as a yes."

As Tanya strolled off, I inhaled the cool evening air tinged with the smoky scent of a neighbor's barbecue. As her rounded figure vanished into the darkness, I left the door ajar in case she'd forgotten anything.

Keith joined me in the hall. "Any messages from Narda?" I asked.

"Negative. No doubt she's too busy cursing my name to anyone who'll listen. Tory return yet?"

"You'd have seen her if she had."

"Does she ever talk about me?" Having a drink tends to loosen Keith's tongue. Like me, he'd limited himself to one, as far as I'd observed.

"Only in a professional capacity."

"How long do you suppose she'll hold a grudge?"

The quarrel we'd just witnessed must have stirred up thoughts of his and Tory's breakup last year. He still didn't seem to recognize how deeply he'd hurt my sister-in-law. "For cheating on her with Narda? How does 'until the end of time' sound?"

"Ominous."

"Sadly, yes."

The scream that drifted through the air was so surreal that, for a moment, neither of us reacted. Then I bolted out the door with Keith on my heels.

Tanya. Why the hell had I let her go alone?

Beneath scattered streetlamps, patchy darkness showed me nothing except two or three cars at the curb. No other lights flicked on; most houses were too well insulated for people to hear.

The screaming had stopped. But not before I registered that it issued from my left.

"Tanya!" Powered by adrenaline, I pounded ahead of my friend. There! Bushes rustled on the slope between my street and the Bryerlys'.

"I see it," Keith said grimly, and started upward, scanning with his flashlight.

I knelt beside the figure huddled on the sidewalk. "Tanya? Are you all right?"

"Something hit me in the shoulder. I lost my balance." She struggled to rise.

"Don't move." Even a minor injury can be serious for a pregnant woman. Also, it was possible she'd been shot or stabbed and hadn't yet registered the pain. "Wait for the ambulance." I was already pressing 911.

"Whoever it was, I can't spot them," Keith said, returning. "Miss Nichols, did you see who attacked you?"

"Uh uh." She was shivering. "I didn't notice anyone nearby. Too busy arguing in my head, I guess."

While Keith summoned backup and played his flashlight around the area, I checked Tanya's pulse. Rapid but steady.

"Let's have a look," I said.

Lowering the shoulder of her stretchy top, she presented a shoulder that—illuminated by my phone's flashlight app—appeared reddish but without any penetrating wound.

"Are you dizzy? Nauseated?" I asked. Although she hadn't mentioned a head injury, it paid to be careful.

"Just scared," Tanya's voice squeaked. "I should have listened to you about walking by myself. I guess something fell, like from a tree or something."

There weren't any trees nearby, nor was I ready to consider this an accident. Could Cress have been angry enough to throw something? If she'd been willing to endanger the baby, that changed everything.

"Hey!" Keith swung around. "Who's that?"

I heard it, too, a scuffling noise above us. "Get down, Tanya." I leaned over to shield her.

"What's happening?"

Keith drew his gun. "Police," he shouted. "Identify yourself."

To my surprise, a voice responded promptly. A young, male voice. "It's me."

"Me who?" Keith's flashlight panned across dark, springy hair above a puzzled face.

"I'm unarmed. I mean, except for this," said the intruder, and waved a thick, twisted cane.

The man was Parker Bryerly.

CHAPTER FIFTEEN

"Put the cane down!" Keith commanded.

Cautiously, Parker lowered the walking stick. "I heard a scream and thought I might need a weapon. Oh, hi, Dr. Darcy."

"Hello." I had to force the word out. If he'd attacked Tanya, I'd pound the little creep myself.

"Is this who hit you?" Keith asked Tanya, still huddled on the sidewalk.

"Hit her?" Parker stared at us from beneath a baseball cap emblazoned with the word "Geek." "Of course not. Tanya! You all right?"

At the corner of the street, a flashing light bar marked the arrival of a cruiser. Behind it, my sister-in-law's sedan whipped into our driveway.

"I don't think so," Tanya said. "Whoever it was, they threw something at me."

"You hurt?" he asked.

"A little."

"Damn it!" Parker clenched and unclenched his fists as if longing to take vengeance on the assailant. "Can't you people do anything?"

"What would you suggest?" Keith asked.

Cress's brother gritted his teeth. "Like, figure out what's going on and quit picking on me."

The detective regarded him coolly.

"Okay, I suppose you *are* doing your job." Parker bent to retrieve the cane. "Since you guys are here, I should go. Gran wants this back."

"Don't touch that!" Keith snapped. "It's evidence."

"Of what?" The programmer halted, his expression a study in astonishment. Very convincing, except that he either had the worst timing in history or was very, very good at deception. Nor was this the first time I'd considered that possibility.

"We'll decide that," the detective said.

Mentally, I'll bet he added, *All in the service of picking on you.*

Parker yielded with a shrug. "Please return it to Gran when you're done. She'll be upset if it gets lost again."

"Again?" A subtle tensing of Keith's muscles spoke volumes.

"It kind of vanished for a few days. Weird."

"When?"

"Monday, I think."

"When did she get it back?" I asked.

"Not sure. Thursday—yesterday—I guess."

During my jog on Tuesday, right before I spotted Wes's body, Lenore had complained about having to rely on her walker. Where had her cane been and who had slipped it back into her possession?

Possibly unimportant. Unless it had been used to attack Wes.

When an ambulance arrived, Tanya protested weakly, subsiding once I promised to meet her at the hospital. Keith isolated Parker for questioning and set about organizing a search for the attacker.

129

When Tory strode up, I answered her questions. She didn't comment, but she couldn't have been happy. Her client had surfaced at a crime scene and, again, there might to be evidence against him.

I excused myself to head for the medical center. There, a female officer met Tanya and me to document the injuries. As my patient had indicated, her shoulder displayed mild bruising, plus there was a small contusion on the hip where she'd fallen. Her vitals and the baby's heartbeat were normal, her blood pressure slightly elevated.

"I'd like to admit you overnight for observation," I said. The fact that she lived alone and had no family in the area concerned me more than ever. Her closest relative, her sister Shana, lived in New York.

Tanya acquiesced reluctantly, adding, "Do you think Cress did this? Would she really try to hurt me and Georgie?"

"I prefer not to jump to conclusions." Especially since those conclusions might throw into question whether Cress was fit to take custody of the baby.

"The thing is..." The surrogate ran a hand over her bulge. "I'm pretty sure I wasn't the first woman Wes cheated with."

I'd suspected as much from the sensuality of his photos and his attitude toward women, such as holding my nurse's gaze a moment longer than most men would. But Tanya's remark sounded specific. "What do you mean?"

"He kept after me to sleep with him again," she said. "He told me he'd broken up with another woman because she couldn't hold a candle to me."

The saying that hell hath no fury like a woman scorned added another dimension to this case. "Did he indicate who it was?"

"No. I didn't ask, either."

A short time later, after checking a few other patients, I

went to confirm Tanya was settled in her room. In the corridor, I ran into Duncan, toting a camera case.

"I heard about what happened." The chubby fellow, whose skin bore the scars of adolescent acne, kept his voice low as we stood outside her room. "Is she okay?"

Privacy law didn't allow me to release medical information to anyone the patient hadn't specified. Moreover, at the moment, I had no idea who could be trusted, including Duncan. "I'm sure she's upset."

"That's understandable, on a lot of levels," the photographer said. "Especially since... I mean, I never had anything against Wes. Yeah, it wasn't fair that some clients chose him over me because of his looks, but that's just business. Only, the way he treated Tanya was disgusting. Not to mention his poor wife."

"She told you the whole story?"

"Yeah." He glanced toward her room. "They find out who did this?"

"Not yet."

"I hope they nail the bastard," he said. "Okay if I go in?"

Despite Tanya's willingness to confide in Duncan, I had major concerns about allowing access to a paparazzi. "How did you know she was here?"

He blinked. "She, uh, texted me."

"Did she ask you to come?"

"No, but I figured she could use the support."

"As her doctor, I urge you to confine your support to texting for the time being," I told him. "She needs rest."

After a brief hesitation, Duncan acquiesced. "I'll let her know I stopped by."

"By text?"

"That's what I meant."

To be on the safe side, I waited until he left before I, too, departed. In my car, I called Keith to let him know Tanya had been admitted. He promised to stop by later to interview her in more depth.

"Not too late," I said. "She should sleep."

"Yeah." Easy to picture my friend rubbing the corded muscles on the back of his neck. "Me, too."

"No rest for the weary."

"Or the wicked."

It was after midnight. I found Tory in the upstairs library/game room with her feet up and bottle of beer in hand.

My sister-in-law proved willing to share what she'd learned while searching for the attacker. She'd persuaded Keith to accept her aid due to her familiarity with the neighborhood.

While no one had been spotted, the police hadn't left entirely empty-handed. "They collected a rock with fibers that might match what Tanya was wearing," she said. "That would support the idea someone threw it at her. They're examining it for DNA and fingerprints."

I sank into an armchair. Aside from the addition of a large-screen TV and videogame system, the room remained much as it had been during my childhood. Books and travel mementoes filled its wall-mounted shelves, while the scent of leather and a hint of pipe tobacco smoke lingered in the air. I had the sense that my father was sitting just out of sight, listening.

"Anything significant about Parker's cane?" I'd been wondering about that.

On the couch, Tory uttered an unladylike burp. "With that ripple design, it's consistent with unusual marks on Wes's body." She didn't explain how she'd run across that information.

"Did they arrest Parker?" To me, the weight of evidence against him seemed heavy. However, my impression of how these things worked was sketchy.

"They released him," she said.

"Seriously?"

"His sister and great-grandmother confirmed they were with him when they heard Tanya scream."

Family members had a built-in bias as witnesses. Also, Cress's statement had provided herself as well as Parker with an alibi. Still, that didn't preclude them both being innocent.

If she hadn't gone after Tanya, that meant they could still reconcile. I believed the strong bond between the women was important to them both, as well as to baby Georgie's future.

"Thanks for the update," I said. "What movie did you see?" I didn't ask what friends had accompanied her, although I was curious.

She named the latest action film.

"How was it?"

"Good stuff. Car chases, shootouts, explosions," Tory said. "But I heard the real explosion went off here."

"In a manner of speaking."

"Details," she commanded.

I described the argument between Cress and Tanya.

"What about the other blowup?" Tory inquired after I finished.

"Which...?"

"Narda." She smiled. "Keith was grumbling big time. I gather she got mad, but not mad enough to return a five-hundred-dollar necklace."

"She'd have preferred a key to his apartment," I said.

"I never figured they'd last." Tory didn't bother to hide her satisfaction. However, she didn't dwell on the subject. "You going to Wes's funeral tomorrow?"

"Not planning to." I doubted anyone would miss me. Or maybe I just wished they wouldn't. "I'll stay home and catch up on loose ends."

"And miss all the excitement?" she joked.

"What excitement? It's a funeral, for goodness' sake."

The instant the words left my mouth, I realized I'd tempted fate again. While I hadn't tacked on "what's the worst that could happen?", I'd implied as much.

Providence granted me a ten-minute reprieve. Then Cress called.

"Dr. Darcy, I apologize for throwing a hissy fit at your house," she said after greeting me.

"Don't worry about it, Cress."

Tory leaned forward. If she'd been a pooch, her ears would have pricked.

"The police said someone assaulted Tanya." My caller spoke with rushed urgency. "How is she?"

As the baby's intended mother, Cress had the surrogate's written consent for me to share medical information. "Bruised. No serious injury."

"She isn't in labor?"

"Not yet."

"I'm glad she's all right. She must be shook up," Cress said. "Surely she doesn't think I had anything to do with it."

"I believe it entered her mind."

"I would never! And neither would Parker," she insisted. "You'll be at Wes's funeral tomorrow, won't you?"

"I... " *...would rather be almost anywhere else.*

"Please come. I need to talk to you. Alone."

"We're talking now," I observed.

"I'm at my parents' house," Cress said. "I can never tell if someone's listening."

Which someone, and for what purpose? Aloud, I asked, "Is your brother staying with you?"

"Yeah. The family has closed ranks," she replied. "So I'll see you tomorrow?"

"I'll be there." As I rang off, I could have sworn I heard the distant laughter of the fates.

Or perhaps it was Tory, chuckling behind her hand.

CHAPTER SIXTEEN

The attack on Tanya Nichols headlined Saturday's edition of *The Safe Harbor Journal*. Soraya's bylined article mentioned that the victim was the Choates's surrogate and implied a connection to Wes's murder.

I resented the speculation. It wasn't my patient's fault she'd agreed to carry a baby for a man who got murdered. Unless, that is, his death had been retribution for his infidelity with her, something that, mercifully, the article did *not* imply.

As for the police, they released a noncommittal statement about the investigation of both crimes moving forward, coupled with a request for any witnesses to Friday night's assault to contact them.

At the hospital, the administrator assured me that security was on alert for suspicious persons and reporters. However, I discovered that neither they nor the officer posted outside Tanya's room for her protection had kept Duncan Axelrod from her bedside.

"The patient approved him, Dr. Darcy," the officer explained after I peered inside and questioned his presence.

"You do realize he's a news photographer?"

"That isn't my call."

"You're right." Although neither of us had the authority to ban a visitor okayed by the patient, his return grated on me. Yesterday, Duncan had respected my request to stay away. His compliance hadn't lasted long.

In the room, both people greeted me. Hanging onto my temper, I asked Duncan to step outside.

His expression tightened. "I don't see why that's necessary. She's been resting all night."

"I think the doctor wants to examine me," Tanya said.

"Oh!" Blushing, he hurried out.

"He isn't dangerous," Tanya cautioned when we were alone.

"Has he photographed you in bed?" I might be overprotective, but since her split with Cress, she had no one to guard her interests. And, as Lenore had remarked, I'd helped put her into this situation.

"He wouldn't exploit me like that." When I didn't comment, she added, "No, he hasn't. And thanks for being my friend, Eric."

I relented. After all, Tanya was a grown woman capable of evaluating her companions. "Of course. Now let's find out how you're doing."

Aside from bruises and a little stiffness, my patient proved to be in fine condition. As for the attack, she confirmed that she'd talked to Keith but couldn't recall any further details.

After promising to sign her release papers, I cornered Duncan in the hall. "Tanya needs a friend and I appreciate the fact that you're filling that role," I began.

"No problem." He brushed a wing of hair from his forehead.

"However, let's be frank. You're a member of the media. If you take advantage of her, I will urge the D.A. to charge you with interfering in a police investigation." I had no idea whether the D.A. would listen to me. Nor did it matter as long as the threat had the desired effect on the photographer. "Is that clear?"

"Yes, doc." His pale gaze remained steady. "I really care about Tanya."

"Good to hear."

Despite misgivings, I left my patient in his company. No sense fighting her wishes.

As I went home to change for the service, my thoughts drifted ahead. How sad that Cress couldn't speak freely around her family. Did she have evidence implicating her brother? Thus far, her faith in Parker had seemed unshakable.

I could hardly complain about having to attend, considering the extent to which I'd been sticking my nose into other people's business. Also, on further consideration, it did seem only courteous.

The Loving Arms Funeral Home occupied a low adobe structure. Its parking lot, shared with a shopping strip, had been divided by cones, with a guard checking ID and admitting only those on his list to the most convenient slots.

Beyond that zone clustered photographers, minicam operators and reporters. No sign of Duncan.

Too bad my town didn't have a drive-through mortuary, I reflected as I showed my driver's license to the guard. I'd heard about one in Los Angeles, which made paying one's respects more convenient. Also, it was easier to avoid getting shot, which I'd heard was a problem at gang funerals. I'd encountered none of that in Safe Harbor.

As I approached the entrance, Soraya rushed toward me, halting just behind a velvet rope. "Dr. Darcy! How is Tanya Nichols? She didn't lose the baby, did she?" Her false solicitousness did nothing to improve my opinion of her.

"No news is good news," I told her, and went inside. A flower-scented hush reigned in the foyer, where I signed the guest book and took a program.

The small chapel had more than enough space for the scattering of mourners. Aside from the Bryerly household, Tory and Keith, there were fewer than a dozen people, presumably friends of the deceased or employees at the studio and bridal shop. No obvious grieving lovers in dark veils, and no strangers in the family section who might be related to Wes.

Seated beside his sister in the front, Parker was whispering to her. They appeared to be on good terms. Whatever she planned to share with me, I doubted it was any shocking revelations about him.

As I slid into a pew, I reflected that I'd attended too many funerals, including those of both my parents. Not my wife's, though.

After Lydia had fallen or jumped to her death at Masada, the Bureau of Consular Affairs had asked the Safe Harbor Police Department to inform the next of kin. They hadn't been aware that her sister was an officer.

The news had devastated Tory. Keith had comforted her, and she'd pulled herself together well enough to accompany him to my place.

I should have accepted their offer to stay with me. Instead, in shock, I'd sent them away and wandered aimlessly through the house, where I'd fallen on the stairs, broken a leg and sprained my shoulder. As a consequence, I'd had to burden Tory with the job of traveling alone to Israel to bury her sister, following the instructions in Lydia's will.

That had been two years ago. Someday, I intended to visit her grave. But I wasn't ready to say a final goodbye yet.

At the front of the chapel, the minister moved to the microphone. He welcomed us and continued earnestly, "At thirty-three, Westlake Choate had just begun to fulfill his potential as an artist, a husband and a father-to-be." He went on to hit the appropriate somber notes and express the hope that forgiveness toward his killer might be possible.

I imagined Wes's spirit watching in disbelief at this sudden end to his life, right before a gallery exhibit intended to boost his reputation as an art photographer. "The paths of glory lead but to the grave" remained as true today as when Thomas Gray composed "Elegy Written in a Country Churchyard" two and a half centuries ago.

Wes had taken only a few steps on the path toward whatever glory he'd dreamed of. No matter how selfish he'd been, he hadn't deserved to die.

The ceremony concluded without any personal tributes. I understood Cress's abstention, in view of the revelation about her husband's cheating. People who have affairs rarely consider the ripple effect of their infidelity, that this disloyalty recasts every declaration of love and every tender moment as a lie. Nor did the program mention a gathering afterwards.

Cress arose shakily on her brother's arm. When her eyes locked with mine, she indicated a side door.

I caught Tory's frown. Keith, who'd positioned himself where he could scan the foyer, didn't notice.

Cress met me in a room decorated in soothing shades of blue-gray, with reproductions of pastoral scenes on the walls. She remained standing, and I followed her lead.

"Is Tanya okay?" She held onto the back of a vintage chair. "She isn't in labor, is she?"

"No." Uncertain whether their agreement to share medical information still applied, I left it at that.

Cress smoothed her black dress, a V-neck design worn without jewelry save for her wedding ring. "I'm sorry I yelled at her. Although she did sleep with my husband. That's a horrible thing to do."

"She regrets it." I stopped there. Not my job to defend Tanya.

"I left her a voicemail." The young widow stared toward a window that overlooked the boulevard. On this side of the building, we were mercifully out of sight of the press. "She hasn't answered."

Wondering why she'd asked me here, I awaited a clue.

"I miss her," the young woman burst out. "She's my best friend. Her betrayal hurt almost as much as my husband's."

"You've been friends a long time." They'd met in college, they'd told me.

"Ten years. Longer than I knew Wes." Cress licked her lips. "The more I think about it... Remember what I told you about Wes bringing me little gifts like we were newlyweds?"

I did.

"I assumed it was to compensate for being wrapped up in his work," Cress said. "Now I think it was guilt. That he was having affairs and buying me off. Was I really that stupid?"

"You trusted the man you loved," I said.

She rushed on. "I don't want to lose my child because of him. Tanya won't really fight me over Georgie, will she?"

I hadn't discussed custody with her and I didn't intend to do so with Cress, either. While the legal outcome would most likely be in Cress's favor, I would much prefer for them to patch things up. "You were supposed to be her birth partner," I reminded her. "You should discuss those arrangements with her."

"You're right. I can't let her down." Cress inhaled rapidly several times. "And it isn't true that I only agreed for her to be the surrogate because of Wes. I was thrilled that she offered to carry our baby."

"You should be telling this to her, not me," I said. "And you should reassure her that you still love the baby after what she and Wes did."

Cress gaped at me. "Of course I do! My gosh, she's worried

141

about that?"

I nodded.

"Thank you, Dr. Darcy." She extended her hand.

I shook it. "Good luck."

In the hall, her brother was waiting. I exited behind them into a blast of hot air.

While the Bryerlys were entering their limousine, Agatha scowled at the reporters. Yet for an instant, I could have sworn the care provider's gaze met Soraya's and held for an instant. Pure chance? Personal enmity? Or something else?

Next to Agatha, Lenore waved at me gaily. "Hi, Dennis! How y'all doing?"

I struggled not to smile at her exuberance. "My condolences, Mrs. Bryerly."

Still no Duncan in the throng of photographers. Perhaps he was serious about putting Tanya ahead of opportunism.

As I waited on the front patio for the crowd to clear, Tory strolled up. "What did the widow have to say?"

"I'd like to hear, too." It was Keith, his eyes red-rimmed from the harsh sunlight and the long hours he'd been working.

"Nothing germane to the case," I told them.

"I'll decide that," Keith said.

"It was private," I responded. "We discussed a medical matter." Which was true, since it concerned the surrogacy.

They both folded their arms and narrowed their eyes as if they'd rehearsed it. "Leave the investigating to the police," Keith said.

"Eric, you care too much about this case," Tory put in.

"I care too much about a lot of things." Such as that my best friend of more than twenty years was stressing out. And that my sister-in-law was gnawing her cuticles to the quick. "I know what we should do about it."

"What do you mean, we?" Keith demanded.

Surly Surrogate

I told him. For once, he couldn't refuse.

CHAPTER SEVENTEEN

"That was a dumb way to call in a favor," Tory told me as several children raced past us on the beach, kicking up sand. "Keith owed you more. Having Narda's party at your house was a major pain in the ass."

Afternoon sunshine burned across my shoulders. Despite a liberal application of sunscreen, I suspected I'd pay for this jaunt, but it was worth it. After the jolts of the past week and the gloom of a funeral, the smell of salt air and the rumble of the Pacific Ocean had a cleansing effect on my spirit. "The food was great. At Keith's expense, too."

"Incoming!" she warned.

Hanging onto my soda can, I lunged for the Frisbee thrown by the topic of our conversation. "Point!" Keith yelled past a stretch of female sunbathers ogling his bare torso and muscular legs.

"I caught it," I protested.

"Spilled your soda," he replied jauntily. "If you'd missed it, that would be two points for me."

"Oh. Right." Not that anyone but him was keeping score in our impromptu, three-way game.

We'd all needed a break, and to lure my friends, I'd called in the favor Keith had promised in return for the loan of my house. Using up the favor on such a minor matter wasn't much of a sacrifice on my part. He'd never have conceded anything important, and if I'd waited too long, we'd both have forgotten it.

Lacking the size and impact of neighboring beaches like those in Huntington and Newport, Safe Harbor's strand attracts mainly a local crowd. On a Saturday afternoon in August, colorful umbrellas and towels dotted the expanse where families watched over romping kids, while young men and women sunbathed and flirted.

Despite my best efforts, I couldn't help registering Tory's gleaming skin and the curves displayed by her bikini. Keith had scanned her with open appreciation when we met in the parking lot, but he'd had the good sense not to comment.

"You going to throw that thing or what?" my sister-in-law demanded, backing away until more distance separated us.

"He's stuck in his head," taunted Keith, occupying a more or less equidistant point. "Egghead Eric."

That had been one of my nicknames in junior high, along with the sarcastic "The Hulk," because I was such a puny specimen. By high school, I'd gained six inches, twenty pounds and a measure of respect.

I took a final gulp from my can and, without warning, shot the Frisbee toward Keith. He'd have caught it except for an inconvenient hole in the sand dug by a toddler, who let out a shriek as my friend tripped and fell, barely missing him.

"Hey!" A heavily tattooed man stalked toward them. "What the hell do you think you're doing?"

Keith levered himself upright. "You okay, little guy?"

The boy nodded.

"Sorry," Keith told the irate father.

"Look where you're going, asshole. Beach is fulla kids." The stranger braced as if for a fight. When none ensued, he swaggered back to his group with barely a glance at his son, who resumed digging furiously.

Growing up with two older brothers, Keith had developed a keen sense of how to pick his battles. Also, as a police officer, he had a duty to uphold the peace, not shatter it.

Since he'd nearly injured the child, he'd been in the wrong. Nevertheless, I resented the tattooed guy's attitude. Always did hate bullies.

Keith tried unsuccessfully not to limp as he approached us. "Let's call it a day," he said.

Since he'd dropped his soda can and missed the Frisbee, he'd clearly lost the match on points. "I declare Tory the winner," I said.

"Fine with me," Keith muttered. "Since I'm on the disabled list."

"You're a mess." Tory reached out to brush sand off his stomach. Fingers curling, her hand halted inches away.

For a charged moment, the ex-lovers locked gazes. They were interrupted by a young blonde woman holding the Frisbee. "Is this yours?" she asked Keith.

"Yeah, thanks." He took it with a nod.

The woman lingered. "Bye," Tory told her.

"Yeah. Bye." Off she went.

That flash of possessiveness told me a lot. I wasn't sure I liked the implications. If they got together again, it could reduce the tension in my household. But eventually, I felt certain, there'd be another blast, with unforeseeable consequences.

I hated for the outing to end when we were finally unwinding. "Let's get a beer at the Suncrest Saloon."

Keith rolled his eyes.

"Cops prefer the Corner Tavern," Tory said.

"Or there," I offered.

A phone rang. All three of us fumbled with the protective bags we'd clipped to our waistbands, until we recognized the tone as Keith's.

He swung away from us and covered one ear against the noise of the surf. "Yeah? Hi."

Not a police call, evidently. While he talked, Tory and I collected towels, snacks and a spare Frisbee.

My sister-in-law's glances toward him reinforced my belief that she still had feelings for her ex. If he did, too, was that necessarily a bad thing? Maybe they'd matured enough for a more lasting relationship.

Despite the unanswered questions about my marriage, I still believed that, in the right union, people were stronger together than alone. My parents had loved each other until the day Mom died. That was what I wanted for myself, and for Tory.

Not that I'm naïve. I've been privy to plenty of true confessions after patients contracted sexually transmitted diseases from an outside source and had to inform their spouses. Or when a test or genetic condition revealed that the husband hadn't fathered his wife's baby. Few marriages survived such revelations.

Had Wes lived, would he and Cress have stayed together if she'd learned about his cheating? And based in what Wes had told Tanya, she hadn't been his only lover.

Damn. I couldn't recall if I'd shared that information with Keith.

My friend limped toward us. "Gotta go."

"It's Narda, isn't it?" Tory didn't wait for a reply. "I'm surprised you're even talking to her."

"I figure there's an outside chance she'll return the

necklace." Keith grabbed his towel.

The three of us sauntered toward the parking area, with Tory in the lead. To Keith, I said, "Something I meant to tell you."

"Yeah?"

"According to Tanya, Wes claimed he dropped another woman because of her."

He thought this over. "Didn't she say she only slept with him once? Why would he end another affair for that?"

"I guess he was infatuated," I said. "That's all I know."

If Keith already suspected Wes of having other affairs and was investigating that angle, he didn't disclose it. At his red sports car, he waved farewell with the towel and took off, preoccupied, I presumed, with the encounter ahead.

Tory and I continued on toward our vehicles. "Wanna bet twenty bucks on whether they break up or have sex?" she asked.

I had no interest in betting. "Could be both."

"Wouldn't surprise me. They're such alley cats." If disappointed by Keith's departure, she hid it beneath cynicism.

"Any plans for tonight?"

"Dad and I enrolled in a bear-building workshop at the toy store," she said.

"Honestly?" I could picture my father-in-law doing something like that, but not Tory. Except out of affection for Morris.

"He's still anxious from that stowaway in the van. He'll enjoy costuming a bear." She adjusted the headband that held frizzy hair off her face. "Want to join us?"

"Tempting, but no."

"I have it on good authority there's a story time, too." She grinned.

"I'll pass."

And so it was that I finally had a chance to do my favorite thing on a Saturday night: nothing at all.

*

For a change, fate left me alone. I enjoyed a long, peaceful stretch of reading, watching videos and sleeping until Sunday morning. Then the newspaper hit my driveway.

Soraya had scored another headline. Her story claimed the surrogate in the Westlake Choate murder was planning to keep the baby. The accompanying picture of a very pregnant Tanya had been shot from the side.

The absence of a photo credit didn't allay the burst of fury I felt toward Duncan. He'd sworn not to exploit her, and now this.

Anyone could have shot that picture. And the tip might have come from elsewhere. But if not Duncan, who?

Maybe someone aware of the family's secrets. Someone who had access to Parker's phone and knife the night of the dinner party. Someone who might have thrown that rock at Tanya directly below the Bryerly house.

There weren't a lot of suspects to choose from, unless you bought into that wild speculation about a super-clever criminal. The only people in attendance the previous Sunday night had been members of the family: Noah, Bianca, Lenore, Cress and Parker. Plus Tanya, Agatha the caretaker and Morris as caterer.

What was I missing? Lenore's rambling clues about events in the past, ranging from eight to fifty-odd years ago, failed to form any identifiable pattern. More likely, Wes had been killed for his faithlessness, or by a greedy, resentful member of his birth family from Oklahoma who'd tried to extort money. But that didn't explain the text on Parker's phone.

In my frustration, I would have tossed out the newspaper after breakfast, except that Morris hadn't read it yet. Sundays being his day off, he'd slept late, leaving a teddy bear in a chef's costume on the counter next to a panda in a police uniform. He and Tory must have enjoyed their workshop.

At my leisure, I dressed for the gallery exhibit. The preview for invited guests started at three o'clock, two hours ahead of the public opening.

As I descended the stairs, mouth-watering scents greeted me from the kitchen. Morris, in striped pajamas, was making crepes, transferring the delicate pancakes into a second pan managed by my brother-in-law. From the back, Barry had the same short frame as his father, only thinner and with more hair on top. Deftly, he sprinkled powdered sugar onto a crepe and folded it with surgical precision, added a fruit filling and folded it again.

Too bad I'd already eaten. "Wish you'd had those ready earlier."

"They reheat." Barry set the crepe on a partially filled plate. "They're better fresh, though." He wiped his hands on his apron. "Hey, can I have a word?"

"Sure."

My brother-in-law faced me across the counter. "Tory won't discuss the investigation, so I'm asking you. Are they going to arrest Parker?"

I couldn't claim inside knowledge, but I respected him too much to offer false assurances. "The evidence keeps mounting. Have you considered the possibility that your friend actually did this?"

Barry shook his head. "Parker and I have been buddies since elementary school. I've seen him yell at people, and I suppose he could throw a punch if you pushed him far enough, but this is different. From what I've read, Wes's murder was calculated and vicious."

"That's my impression, too," I conceded. "But neither of us

150

is exactly unbiased about Parker." Nor was Cress, who knew her brother better than either of us.

"He'd never survive prison. And he doesn't deserve it. Parker's the most loyal person I've ever met." Barry spoke with unaccustomed intensity. "He's beside himself with worry about his family. His sister, of course. His grandmother, too. He's afraid the stress might harm her."

"She's his great-grandmother," I corrected automatically.

"And his dad," Barry went on. "Parker says his dad's losing it."

Noah Bryerly had struck me as smoothly in control. "In what way?"

"Parker thinks he might be developing dementia like his great-whatever-she-is." At a snap from behind him, Barry glanced at Morris, but it was only a bit of butter protesting in the pan.

"What are his symptoms?" While I'd witnessed nothing of concern, my interactions with Noah had been limited.

"According to Parker, his dad's lost his coding skills. He could never have founded a software company with the abilities he has now."

Parker and Cress's father was in his late fifties, young to be developing Alzheimer's. However, some poor souls suffer from an early onset of the disease. And that's only one of many conditions we term dementia, each with a different cause and prognosis.

"Considering that he left the field decades ago, that doesn't necessarily indicate a problem," I said. "Still, Parker should urge his father to be tested. If he does have a disorder, treatment might slow or halt the progression." In the last few years, research into brain function and neurological diseases had proceeded at a feverish pace.

"That's a good idea. Should have thought of it myself." As a urologist, Barry is an excellent diagnostician. "I had kind of a one-track focus on the murder investigation."

As long as we were on the subject of Noah Bryerly, I asked, "By the way, did Parker's father ever smoke?"

That had been, Tory and I had speculated, where Bianca had picked up the previously despised habit. Smoking has also, I've read, been shown to double the risk of Alzheimer's.

"Not that I'm aware of. But that's another thing. Parker's concerned his mother's smoking herself into an early grave."

"She's strongly addicted to cigarettes," I agreed.

"So is that Greek woman," Morris put in. He'd been so quiet, I'd forgotten he could hear every word.

"Agatha?"

"Yes, her. I had to kick her out of the Bryerlys' kitchen last Sunday," he said. "Cigarette smoke can affect the taste of the food."

We waited, but he added nothing. "Eric, can you tell me anything else about Parker?" Barry asked.

"I'm afraid not. Keith doesn't discuss his findings with me." Our only contact since yesterday had been a text in response to my query about Narda, in which he'd noted, "Got the necklace." Terse and to the point.

I checked my watch. Should have left five minutes ago.

"I'm holding you up. Sorry," said my brother-in-law.

"No problem."

But my lateness proved to be more of an inconvenience than anticipated. Normally, you wouldn't find a crowd swarming to visit the commercial strip that housed the Wine Arts Gallery. Today, TV news vans and other vehicles packed the lot, forcing me to leave my car halfway down the block.

As I approached on foot, a cluster of reporters and videocam operators blocked my view of the gallery's glass front. Only when I got closer did I spot the central attraction of their impromptu news conference.

Arm in arm, Cress and Tanya were facing their tormentors. In defiance of good sense, they'd apparently decided to tackle the rumors head-on.

Judging by their panicked expressions, they were losing the battle.

CHAPTER EIGHTEEN

"Dr. Darcy!" Cress's frantic cry resulted in a ripple of movement as the ladies and gentlemen of the press swung toward me.

Instinctively preparing for combat, I squared my shoulders. From the sidelines, Tory gave me a sardonic thumbs-up. Nearby, Keith's forehead puckered, which I took as a warning of sorts.

Say as little as possible. Yeah, I got that.

A path cleared for me. I joined the two women in front of the display window, which featured several large nature photos and a sign announcing the Westlake Choate Memorial Exhibit, billed as "Secrets and Shadows." Now, there was an appropriate theme.

"We've been trying to convince them we're still friends," Tanya explained.

"And I'm her birthing partner," Cress added. "Everything's on track."

"Then why won't you answer the question?" demanded Hayden O'Donnell, the TV reporter with the square face.

"Yes, Miss Nichols." In a form-fitting black dress and wide-brimmed hat, Soraya Montenegro made a dramatic fashion statement. "Is this your baby or Mrs. Choate's? Or are you planning to raise it together?"

Two feminine mouths trembled and their linked arms tightened. For heaven's sake, why hadn't it occurred to them to clarify this point before they went public?

"Inside," I told them. "This is a bad idea."

"We want them to stop harassing us," Tanya protested. "Can't they see we're just ordinary people?"

"There's nothing ordinary about your situation," responded a woman holding a microphone. "Everybody knows who's the daddy. But who's the mommy?"

That served as a cue for Hayden and the others to target me. "You're the expert, Dr. Darcy," the man said. "What's the law here?"

I nearly responded that I was an obstetrician, not a lawyer. On the other hand, if I focused on the legal aspects, maybe my patients would be struck by a bolt of common sense and get the hell out of here.

"California has among the best-established and most liberal surrogacy laws in the world," I began.

My patients remained planted on the walkway, gaping at me. My mental command to leave had zero impact. As for Keith, he frowned at my foolishness in revealing more than absolutely necessary. Well, I wasn't a police officer.

"What happens if there's a disagreement over custody?" someone called. "Does it wind up in the courts?"

"Anybody can sue anyone over anything," I replied. "But state law has established a parent-child relationship between the intended parents and the child or children of a gestational carrier, regardless of who provided the egg and sperm. In every challenge I'm aware of, courts have upheld assisted reproduction agreements."

I registered Tanya's sharp intake of breath. Did she

seriously think she could keep baby Georgie? Judging by the rigidity in Cress's stance, that remained a concern for her, too.

More questions flew, too fast and overlapping for me to sort out. Luckily, a limousine rolled toward us, its blaring horn startling the reporters. A few dropped their pads and others shrank back.

A uniformed driver stuck his head out his window. "Clear the way, please," he called. "We have a handicapped person who requires access."

Grumbling, the press retreated. Among them, I spotted a young man with a cap pulled low—Duncan Axelrod, his acne scars prominent in the sunlight.

His efforts to wiggle through the gathering toward Tanya met with elbowed resistance from the rest of the media. Halting, Duncan stared around uncertainly. Tanya ignored him.

First to emerge from the limo was Parker Bryerly, to eager murmurs from the press at this fresh prey. Turning, he assisted the heavyset Agatha Kozma, who wore her usual black dress punctuated by a long, colorful scarf. With the temperature rising toward the triple digits, she must have been sweating.

Did the care provider have a low body temperature or was her overdressing the result of previous abuse that left her feeling perpetually unsafe? Or was she hiding bruises, and if so, how had she received them?

You aren't the detective, Eric. Focus on your patients.

Parker offered his hand to his great-grandmother. After retrieving her walker from the trunk, the driver hurried around with it.

In the meantime, a funny thing happened, one of those blink-of-an-eye interactions that might slide by unnoticed. Moving toward the entrance, Agatha stepped on the edge of her scarf and stumbled. The closest person, Soraya, caught her elbow to steady her.

156

Nothing strange about a simple act of kindness except that the two women's heads tilted toward each other and Soraya murmured something that sounded to me like, "I can't afford to lose you."

Excuse me, what? The reporter and Lenore's aide were close acquaintances?

I doubt her comment drifted to anyone beyond the immediate bystanders: Parker, Lenore and me. Parker's head jerked up and his eyebrows beetled into a solid line.

Soraya eased back, braying, "Tell us, Parker, how does it feel to see an exhibit dedicated to the man you killed?" I couldn't be sure from his outraged expression whether he was reacting to her question or to her earlier, *sotto voce* remark.

The rest of the media seized on the angle. "How can you show your face in front of the surrogate after attacking her?" someone demanded.

And another: "Were you trying to kill your brother-in-law's baby? Isn't it enough that you're accused of his murder?"

In the lull that followed, a quavery but forceful voice rang out. "Nobody's accused him of anything, except for you numbskulls!" declared Lenore, rattling her walker. "I accuse all y'all... of being idiots!"

With that parting shot, the angry woman clumped across the sidewalk, her caretaker and her great-grandson scurrying to keep up. I took the opportunity to shepherd Cress and Tanya inside. Since the reception was private, we should be safe from the pack for a while and, with luck, they'd get tired of waiting.

No one else emerged from the limo. Keith and Tory followed our little parade inside.

In the gallery, chill air blasted over us. The contrast to the bright sunlight left me nearly blind, and I paused rather than risk mowing anyone down.

The place smelled like wine, perfume and aftershave lotion.

157

The clink of glasses, the rustle of clothing and the murmur of voices formed a soothing cadence after the shouts of the press.

As my eyes adjusted, I noticed how confined the space was. The gallery occupied what had once been an escrow office, and despite the removal of a wall here in the main room, the low ceiling kept things cozy. The bar along one side and the round tables in the center added not only clutter but also a reminder that the primary source of income was undoubtedly the booze.

I spotted Noah and Bianca Bryerly across the room, chatting with a group of local bigwigs. Through knots of guests, most rather formally dressed for Southern California, wove the gallery's owner, gleefully shaking hands.

In his late thirties with spiky bleached hair, Armand Alton wore a purple trench coat over a white shirt, black silk vest and lavender pants. I tried not to resent the man who, three years ago, had dismissed Lydia's request for an exhibit. He'd contended she was still searching for her voice, and perhaps he'd been right.

Armand had claimed in a later newspaper interview that he loved mentoring artists. That had failed to impress me, since he paid them nothing up front, took a fifty percent commission and expected them to publicize their own shows.

Striving for objectivity about Wes's work, I slowly circled the room. Here in the front gallery, the photos presented an unusual take on nature, capturing the shadows of trees and leaves rather than the objects themselves. Birds appeared in a couple of pictures, reflected in pools of water. In another, a woman stood silhouetted among trees, blending into the play of light and darkness. The impact was stark and riveting.

Cards on the wall contained cryptic titles such as "Nature Abstract Number Eleven," along with steep prices that I guessed had risen since the artist's death.

I moved into the second, smaller room. Here unfolded a

series of naked or partially draped women, viewed from the side or back. Patterns overlaid their bodies like tattoos, fading into billowy backgrounds.

"Do you suppose he slept with all of them?"

I hadn't noticed Tory at my elbow until she spoke. At the reminder of what these pictures implied, my fascination with the exhibit ruptured, as if a silk curtain had been slashed with a knife.

Wes had been granted both vision and charisma, and had used them to prey on women. Who were these models? Had they loved Wes? Had he left them devastated, or boiling with rage?

Disgust seared my chest at his callous betrayals. At the abandonment, the lies and deceptions. The sensation was so fierce, so disproportionate to what I was seeing, that I might have feared I was having a heart attack except I was too mad to admit any distraction.

This wrath had less to do with Westlake Choate than with my marriage, I realized. It had been simmering for years. Since my wife shut me out and flew off, then died without telling me why, as if I meant nothing.

You don't wad people up like tissues and throw them in the trash. If you love someone, you don't act as if you're the only person in the world who matters.

"Eric?" my sister-in-law said. "Are you all right?"

I had no idea what to say. Lydia had hurt her, too. But I couldn't share my pain while it was raw and unexamined.

A speaker crackled and Armand Alton's voice broke over us. "I want to welcome everyone to this sad but joyous occasion in memory of a great talent snuffed out too soon."

Sad but joyous? The absurdity of his remark made me smile in spite of myself, and I noticed Tory relaxing. Either laughing with me, or glad to note that I wasn't in the throes of a seizure.

Most of the people in the small gallery exited to the larger room, attending on the owner as he launched into an amplified account of how he'd met the young photographer and been struck by his gifts. Wes might have relished the praise, but I sensed only reproach from the few who remained near me.

Cress and Tanya stood before the most hurtful, revealing photo. The surrogate's tumble of blond hair and pregnancy-enlarged nude body were unmistakable. Shifting closer, I saw that Wes had caught enough of her partly averted face to reveal the glow of lovemaking.

"I'm sorry." The surrogate spoke softly to Cress. "It was stupid of me to pose for him, and then to let him... I guess the attention flattered me, but that's no excuse for not stopping him. For not stopping myself. I shouldn't have come today. I've just made things worse."

"I asked you to be here." The widow didn't return her gaze, though.

"If I could undo it, if there was any way..."

"Slut." The insult rasped from Agatha, who'd planted herself next to them. She scowled at the adjacent nude picture, as if this black-haired woman rather than Tanya had incurred her revulsion.

"Please stay out of this," Cress said.

"Your family is cuckoo." She pronounced the word "kah-KO," emphasis on the second syllable.

Over the speaker, a smattering of applause greeted some statement of Alton's. I was glad I wasn't trapped in the outer room, forced to pretend interest. On the other hand, despite the A/C, things were getting heated in here.

"You're a fine one to talk," Parker snarled at Agatha. Fists clenched, Cress's brother had shed his usual mellow air. "My family has been nothing but kind to you, and you repay them by tattling to that snake of a reporter. How much is she paying you to sell us out?"

He'd drawn the same conclusion I had: that Agatha was Soraya's inside source. The caregiver must have overheard plenty of personal information, which explained the newswoman's scoops.

"Did you sneak into Dad's van?" Tory demanded. "Trying to cash in by spying on my father?"

I hadn't considered that it might have been Agatha in the van. Since she lived just up the hill, that would explain the intruder's fast disappearance. And I'd run into her minutes later, on the path.

The caretaker rounded on Parker. "You have no idea what you are a part of."

"Yeah? Why don't you explain it to me?" he challenged.

The stocky woman's mouth worked, as if she were considering spilling whatever had provoked her resentment of the Bryerlys. With her usual bizarre timing, Lenore demanded loudly, "Who are all these naked women, anyway?"

Their voices must have carried, because Noah Bryerly strode in. "What's going on? Cress, are you okay?"

"I'm fine, Dad."

"Well, I'm not," Parker said. "Agatha's been snitching about us to that reporter."

Something unreadable flickered in the older man's eyes. However, he said calmly, "Surely there's been a misunderstanding."

Agatha seemed to shrink into her black dress. Still, she summoned the nerve to tell her employer, "You should pay attention to these photographs."

"I'm not a fool."

The laser-sharp look he directed at her indicated that Noah Bryerly hadn't missed an iota of the scandals involving his family. But whatever action might be called for, he did not intend to let her force his hand.

"Suit yourself." Flinging her scarf dramatically around her neck, Agatha turned toward the door. "Your grandmother is tired, and we leave."

"Be careful with that scarf," Parker muttered. "Ever heard of Isadora Duncan?"

Lenore rattled her walker, but not noisily enough to obscure the crack. To me, her behavior showed a lot more sense than her great-grandson did. Issuing a not-very-subtly veiled death threat was a stupid thing for a murder suspect to do.

Especially when the homicide detective had just walked into the room.

CHAPTER NINETEEN

Although Keith's cranky air reminded me that he hated references he didn't understand, he tried gamely to catch up. Indicating the photos, he asked, "Is one of these women Isadora Duncan?"

Oops. I should have clued him in.

"My son was attempting to be funny," Noah told him. "Isadora Duncan was a famous dancer who got killed because of her scarf."

Keith's lower jaw jutted in a bulldog expression worthy of Winston Churchill. "How did that happen?"

"I think she was in an open car," Cress said. "She wore this really long scarf that got tangled in a tire or something."

"Like, in the 1920s," Tanya added.

They must be dance enthusiasts, I thought. Or followers of a website that posted oddities of the past.

"I see." That was Keith's way of dismissing the subject.

"...death is a loss to the entire art-loving world. We all mourn the untimely demise of Westlake Choate." Over the speakers, Armand Alton concluded his speech to loud clapping.

Agatha seized Lenore's arm. "We go home before you

collapse." I wasn't sure what had prompted this remark, since the elderly woman appeared no shakier than usual.

"Hold on." Parker turned to Keith. "Agatha has been leaking information to that local reporter. And she called Tanya a slut, so think about the implications."

I didn't have to. "Did you throw a rock at her?" I demanded of the caregiver. "Did you attack a pregnant woman?"

Faded brown eyes blinked in surprise. "No, doctor. Look closer at the photos."

"The gallery's covered in photos. Which ones?"

"I will let you decide."

Her evasiveness added to my skepticism. If she honestly believed we were missing evidence, she'd spell it out.

"Haven't I been humiliated enough?" Tanya cried. "I apologized to Cress. It's nobody else's business."

Keith cut through the drama. "Mrs. Kozma, have you been providing information about this investigation to Miss Montenegro?"

The stocky woman shrugged. "Maybe a little."

"I asked you not to discuss the case with anyone." Irritation roughened his voice.

"I apologize if I offend." Agatha was dragging Lenore and her walker toward the exit. "I speak too much already. I stop now."

"Loose lips sink ships," Lenore chirped.

I recognized the World War II caution against revealing information that might aid the enemy. My mother used to quote it to encourage discretion on a personal level, but I sensed that the Bryerlys were indeed engaged in a war. What kind of war, I hadn't figured out.

Parker smacked his fist into his palm. "Keith, aren't you going to stop her?"

"Take it easy, son," Noah said.

164

"Dad, she was at our house that night. She could have texted from my phone." He had every right to be angry, in my opinion.

Tory was furious too, judging by her glare at Agatha's retreating figure. Although we hadn't received confirmation, it seemed likely we'd identified my father-in-law's stowaway.

Agatha *had* denied attacking Tanya on the sidewalk. Unless it had been Cress, however, I didn't see who else could have done it.

"Detective Sparks is aware of the circumstances," Noah told his son. "Why don't you escort your sister and Miss Nichols out for a bite to eat?"

Tanya hugged herself. "No, thank you, Mr. Bryerly. I'm tired of people fussing over me."

"Agatha had no business calling you names," Cress put in protectively. "We can see the photos for ourselves. It's no secret what Wes did."

"I'm not sure she was referring to Tanya. This is the one she was staring at." With her cell, Tory took a shot of the black-haired woman's framed image.

"You aren't supposed to take pictures in here." Noah indicated a small sign to that effect.

"Sorry." Tory lowered the cell without deleting anything. "Just being thorough."

"Remember who you work for, Miss Golden," he added.

"I haven't forgotten."

Who was that woman? Had a member of Noah's social circle been among his son-in-law's lovers? Not a pretty situation, no matter how artistically Wes portrayed her. Especially since their affair might have led to his murder by the jealous subject or an outraged husband.

"Detective Sparks, what can we do to help your investigation?" Noah asked.

"You can tell me who that woman is."

"I'm afraid I don't recognize her."

Keith peered after Agatha, but she was gone. Ignoring the prohibition, he clicked a snapshot of the image, too. However, since facial recognition didn't include buttocks and he could hardly ask the female guests to strip naked for comparison, I presumed he'd have to wait for identification until he could re-interview the caretaker or find another witness.

Noah went to rejoin his wife in the main gallery. After Tanya again declined to dine with them, Parker and Cress left together.

I'd had enough of the Bryerlys' secrets and shadows. However, despite my impatience to be alone with my newly discovered anger at my wife, common courtesy prompted me to offer Tanya a lift. She accepted with thanks.

"How are you doing?" I asked as we threaded our way through the front room. Around us, the crowd seemed thicker and louder than before.

"Fine," Tanya said. "I just need to think."

"About the baby?" Or, specifically, about custody.

"Yeah."

I opened the outer door, not paying attention until the sight of a dwindled but fierce knot of reporters brought me up short. Why were they still hanging around in the middle of the afternoon? Surely there must be more important things happening in Southern California.

"Where's Mrs. Choate?" demanded a man with perspiration darkening his shirt. "Was there an argument?"

"No! Go away," Tanya said.

Cress and Parker must have left via a rear exit. I wished I'd thought to do the same.

The clamor intensified. "Dr. Darcy, will you induce labor tonight?"

"Tanya, do you consider this your and Wes's love child?"

"Stop!" Outraged, I raised my hand. "This is a pregnant woman, in case any of you are too dense to notice. Get the f... frick out of her way and go find some real news."

The ladies and gentlemen of the press stared at me as if I'd sprouted horns. I wasn't sure if it was because they'd expected my usual calm demeanor or if they were trying to figure out what I meant by "real news."

I gestured to Duncan, who'd removed his cap. His longish hair hung limp in the heat. "Yes, Doctor?" he said.

"Please drive Miss Nichols wherever she wants to go." With labor likely to start soon, it was best if he stayed with her, despite my reservations about him.

"Okay, Tanya?" the photographer said.

Nodding, she took his arm. The knot of press parted.

"That was quite a performance, doc." Soraya Montenegro scooted to my side. "What's with the personal service? Is Tanya a special patient?" A breeze ruffled the long dark hair spilling from beneath her wide-brimmed hat.

"All my patients are special." Long dark hair. Was that a coincidence? "Did you ever pose for Wes Choate?"

Her mouth curved. "You're joking, right?"

"No, I'm not."

Keith, who'd emerged from the gallery, interjected smoothly, "Miss Montenegro, we need to talk. Please come with me."

For the blink of an eye, she froze. Then a practiced smile dropped into place. "Detective, you can interview me any time." Strutting as if she'd scored a coup, Soraya accompanied him to his car.

"Why did you ask if she'd posed for Westlake, Dr. Darcy?" another reporter asked.

I checked my watch. "The exhibit opens to the public in twenty minutes. See for yourselves if you recognize anyone in the photos." Who could tell? The pests might make themselves useful.

Instead, they'd no doubt copy the picture of Tanya's naked image. I hoped Cress sued their socks off for copyright infringement.

*

At home, I spent over an hour postponing what I had to face. I changed my clothes, ate a snack, read my email and said hello to my father-in-law, who was watching TV in his room.

At last I stood in the upstairs guest room staring at a scene from eight years ago, as transfixed as Agatha had been earlier at the gallery.

When I'd moved the framed photo of our wedding party here after Lydia's death, I'd reasoned that constantly seeing it in my bedroom would be too painful. However, it might also have been healing. Now, the details fired into me like darts.

At the center of the lineup, my petite, intense wife wore the rainbow-hued gown she'd designed herself. Beside her, the tuxedoed groom appeared younger and glossier than the man I saw daily in the mirror. The same was true of Keith, my best man, and, barely reaching his jawline, a formally clad Barry, who'd walked his sister down the aisle.

To Lydia's left towered Tory, her uncomfortable stance reflecting a raw coltishness that had since vanished. Next to her, bridesmaid Shana Nichols—Tanya's sister— posed with a formal smile.

How little we'd known ourselves or where our paths would lead. People say you can't change the past, but they're wrong. When our perceptions change, so does our story.

I forced my gaze back to Lydia. In the years when this picture had hung in the master bedroom, I'd attributed the pensive twist to her lips to regret that her mother couldn't be at the ceremony. Nelle Golden had died five years earlier.

What if Lydia's mood hadn't been about her mother? Maybe she'd been uncertain that she loved me. If so, she should have told me before our wedding. Yes, she'd have broken my heart. Instead, she'd broken my life.

With rising anger came an urge to stomp to the attic and kick a hole in that airy-fairy artwork of children, that testimony to my wife's secrets. To the dream she'd shared with friends but not me. To the guilt and self-blame her silence had cursed me with.

You're overreacting.

Who cares? I'm as entitled to overreact as the next guy.

I was holding conversations with myself. Scary.

Twinges of pain distracted me. My neck muscles had tightened to the point where a headache threatened.

As I flexed my shoulders, it occurred to me that my coping mechanism when dealing with a difficult situation was to do research. Might as well try that.

In the library/game room, I opened my laptop on the coffee table and searched under "abandonment." Up popped a post about children whose parents had left, destroying their sense of security and their self-esteem. I'd been spared that, thank goodness.

In the quiet room where my father used to read his medical journals, I inhaled the reassuring trace of old pipe smoke. Although I'd had to survive my teen years without my mother, my father had been there for me.

As had Lydia. We'd connected in high school, drawn by the mutual sorrow of having lost a parent. We'd shared anguish and fears, lifting each other out of depression and establishing a bond that had matured over the years.

I expanded my search parameter to "spousal abandonment." That brought up a very different queue.

The post that I clicked on provided a level of insight that I badly needed. Sudden abandonment by a husband or wife without clear cause is a violation of trust, the article stated. The pain of betrayal can be more devastating and harder to recover from than a spouse's death.

These past two years, my attempts at healing had centered on my being a widower. Lydia's withdrawal prior to her final, fatal journey had seemed secondary. Also, I'd believed I knew the reason: that she didn't want children.

This week I'd learned otherwise. As far as I could tell, I'd done nothing to drive her away. The woman I'd loved since we were teenagers had left with no explanation and no concern for me at all.

I had no idea where to go from here. What to do with my new awareness or my anger.

A movement in the room startled me. "What the...?"

"Hey, Eric. Glad to see the media didn't eat you alive." Tory dropped onto the couch, stretching her legs atop the coffee table. A lazy grin told me she'd enjoyed my reaction.

Since I was in no temper to share my internal turmoil, I asked, "Find out anything about the mystery woman?"

Tory shrugged. "I wrote a list of black-haired women who might have posed for Wes."

"Anyone I know?" I asked.

"You mean Soraya?" As usual, my sister-in-law was on top of her game. "I ruled her out."

"Why?"

"Her hair is frizzier and finer," Tory said.

Very observant. "Who else is on the list?"

"Narda, for one."

Not impossible, considering that the nurse might have encountered Wes at a wedding or other event. Her spontaneous hook-up with Keith in an on-call room indicated she was sexually venturesome. "Have you mentioned that to

170

anyone?"

"As in our friend on the homicide squad?" she teased. "No. Come on, Eric. If he couldn't recognize his lover's nude back, he's unbelievably clueless."

"Men don't pay a lot of attention to a woman's back."

"Point taken." She fiddled with her cell. "But I think this woman is older than Narda. A bit thicker through the hips, too."

"That could indicate she's given birth," I said.

"Thick hips? Another good reason not to have kids."

"And this leads you to suspect whom?" I probed.

"I have an idea but it's shocking." My sister-in-law eyed me speculatively.

"More shocking than Wes cheating on his wife with their surrogate?" I scoffed.

"Yes," Tory said. "But I'm withholding it for now. I need to dig further into the Bryerlys' background."

Since I wasn't sure how much Barry had told her, I said, "According to your brother, Parker's afraid his father might be showing signs of dementia."

That drew her attention. "In what way?"

"He believes Noah has lost his coding skills."

"That's interesting." Her tone implied the opposite.

On further consideration, I agreed. "Not unusual, considering he's been out of the computer business for decades. And he was certainly on top of the situation at the gallery tonight."

"He seems sharp to me, too," Tory said.

Downstairs, the doorbell chimed. It was followed instantly by loud knocking.

"Sounds urgent." I stood up.

"They'll scare Dad." Tory beat me to the hall.

On the front porch fidgeted a disheveled Parker. He'd shed the suit jacket he'd sported at the exhibit but wore the same shirt, rumpled and splattered with red.

"Tory, thank God you're home," he said. "I had to... I can't..."

"Breathe," she commanded. "What happened?"

Parker's hands chopped the air. "Agatha's dead. Someone strangled her with her scarf. On the patio. Oh, God."

"Did you call the police?"

"Not yet. I panicked."

Tory plucked the cell from her pocket. "Come inside and we'll..."

"And Gran!"

My heart nearly stopped. "Lenore? What about her?"

"She's missing," Parker said.

CHAPTER TWENTY

Missing but not dead. As Parker entered the house, my heart rate slowed, but only by a fraction. The prospect of Lenore at the mercy of a killer revolted me.

As did the strangulation of Agatha. Although she'd tattled on her employers and violated their trust, she hadn't deserved a ghastly death.

On the phone, Tory was filling in the dispatcher. I heard Keith's name as well as Parker's, but my worries drowned out her voice. Did the murderer have Lenore or had she escaped? Was she wandering helpless and terrified?

After Tory clicked off, she told our guest, "Stay here. The police want to talk to you."

Parker began to pace. "I have to call my sister. Cress just dropped me off. Thank God she didn't come in with me. What if the killer's still around? I'd better warn Mom and Dad."

As he reached into his pocket, Tory tapped his arm. "First, call your lawyer."

"It's Sunday night. Lawyers don't work on Sundays."

"As a defense attorney, it's his job to be here."

Slowly, Parker yielded. "Okay."

"This is a different M.O. from Wes's murder," Tory observed

to me while her client spoke into his cell. "It didn't require as much physical strength and I doubt it was planned."

Had a different person done this? Was it because Agatha had recognized someone in the photo who didn't dare be identified, or because she'd snitched on the Bryerlys?

The obvious suspect was, again, Parker. He'd railed at her at the gallery, and he'd found the body.

He finished his conversation. "Mr. Noriega advised me not to talk to the police until he gets here."

"Good advice," Tory said flatly. Her instincts as a former police officer must be screaming at her, but she worked for Parker's family now.

"Lenore has a habit of wandering off," I reminded them. "Maybe she was gone when this happened. I should go search for her."

"The police put out a BOLO." That, I'd learned, was cop talk for Be On The Lookout. Tory waved us toward the kitchen. "Coffee?"

"Thanks." Parker peered down at his shirt. "I should clean up."

As one, Tory and I shouted, "No!"

"Huh?" He blinked so hard, it's a wonder his contacts didn't dislodge. "Oh, that would make me look guilty, right?"

"What is that?" I indicated the red stains.

"Eric, he shouldn't discuss this," Tory cautioned.

"Arrabbiata," Parker blurted.

"What's that?" she asked.

"Spicy spaghetti sauce. Cress and I ate at Papa Giovanni's." He perched on a stool at the counter. "Mr. Noriega didn't say not to talk to you guys."

"You should save the details." Tory moved to the coffeemaker.

Abruptly, I recalled something. "Tory, did you tell the

dispatcher that Lenore has a tracking device in her watch?"

"No. I wasn't aware that she did." My sister-in-law poured water into the device.

"That's the weird thing," Parker said, as if this entire day hadn't been weird. "When I went into Gran's room to look for her, she'd left her watch on the dresser."

Either she'd fled and was afraid of being tracked, or the killer/kidnapper had forced her to leave it. That would mean he or she knew about the device.

"Does she carry a phone?" Tory took out a canister of coffee. While Morris grinds his beans fresh, she and I are too lazy.

"Gran doesn't have one."

I couldn't sit here while Lenore might be wandering around in the twilight. If she were hiding, perhaps the sight of me would draw her out.

"I'd better search," I said. "But let me get you a change of clothes, Parker. The police will need to take yours."

"Don't remove them until they've seen and photographed you wearing them," Tory advised.

"I can pick up fresh clothes at home," he protested.

"Your parents' house is a crime scene," Tory noted as the coffee machine began burbling. "And I doubt you'll be returning there or to your apartment for hours. That reminds me. Hold out your arms."

"Okay." With a puzzled frown, Parker extended his bare forearms on the counter.

Tory snapped pictures of both sides as well as his hands. "What's your opinion, Eric? You see any bruising? Cuts or abrasions?"

I checked. "No." While he wouldn't necessarily have been injured while strangling Agatha, there ought to be some redness on his palms. There wasn't.

"Good to have a doctor's opinion," she said.

"I didn't do it, but somebody did." Parker shuddered. "When I heard about Wes, it didn't seem real. I mean, his body in a swamp. What the hell is that? But this. Agatha, crumpled and blotchy on our patio. She loved that scarf. To kill her with it was just wrong."

Leaving him with Tory, I mounted the stairs and riffled through my closet. Parker was skinnier than me and several inches shorter. I settled on a pair of jeans and a plain T-shirt.

As I removed them from the hangers, I heard sirens bouncing off the bluffs. Through the rear window of the bedroom, I glimpsed the blue and red whirl of emergency lights in the dusk, but didn't have a clear view. The Bryerly house was too high and at an angle.

They had a pretty good view of my house, though, I recalled. Was Lenore hiding nearby, watching for me?

I hurried down, handed over the clothes, and went outside. No sense driving. If Lenore lingered in the area, she'd be on foot.

I'd scarcely reached the sidewalk when a black sedan halted. Keith emerged with the frazzled air of a man who needs to be in too many places at once. "Leaving?" he asked.

"To look for old Mrs. Bryerly," I told him.

He glanced upward to where the red lights flashed, then back to me. "Parker's at your house?"

"With Tory. Lawyer on the way." While I doubted my friend would share details, I had to try. "Any luck talking to Soraya?"

Weariness eroded the stony expression he usually wore on the job. "In future, she should be more careful who she uses as a source."

Would Soraya feel remorseful when she learned of Agatha's murder, or simply disappointed at losing an informant? That depended on whether the reporter had a heart, I supposed.

We parted, Keith to do his job and me to stride along the sidewalk, hoping to glimpse a puffy white coif and hear a reedy voice declare, "Dennis, honey! How y'all doing?"

The only noises that reached me were the chatter of emergency workers, the far-off rumble of the ocean and a few windows scraping open as neighbors indulged their curiosity. No rattle of a walker or tap of a cane.

I paid scant attention to ordinary sights: a couple walking a dog, a cat slinking into the bushes. My thoughts strayed instead to the crime scene on the bluff above. Ruling out a random home invader as too much of a coincidence, I assumed the killer had been among those present at last Sunday night's dinner. Mentally, I reviewed the list as well as their whereabouts tonight.

Parker and Cress. They'd left the gallery and dined together, thus providing each other with alibis aside from a narrow window of opportunity after he returned to the house.

Noah and Bianca. From fragments of conversation at the exhibit, I had the impression they'd planned to go out with a group of local notables, including the mayor and her husband. Easily confirmed.

My father-in-law. While he'd catered the dinner, I'd seen Morris in his room around the time of tonight's murder. Plus, he had no motive, except resentment if he believed Agatha had sneaked into his van to eavesdrop.

Tanya had been upset when Agatha yelled "Slut!" But she presumably was hanging out with Duncan.

Lenore had once joked that her family couldn't put her in a retirement home because she knew too much. But she hadn't explained what she meant, and, besides, her memory was too unreliable to be credible.

Could she have killed the caretaker in self-defense or in a fit of confusion? Dementia can cause aggressive behavior in a normally nonviolent person.

At the ring of my cell, I snatched it from my pocket. The screen read "Cress Choate."

I answered. "Are you okay?"

"Parker told me Agatha's dead. I can't believe it." Her voice trembled. "Is Gran okay? Have you found her?"

"Not yet." I was touched that she'd asked if I, rather than the police, had located Lenore. "The detectives will need to talk to you."

"I'm on my way to the hospital," she answered. "Tanya's in labor."

Tonight, of all nights. I shifted into obstetrician mode. "How far apart are the pains?"

"Um..." Her voice trailed off as she repeated my question to someone. "Eighteen minutes," Cress relayed.

"She's in the early stage." That part of labor can last as long as twenty hours, especially for a first-time mother. "Are the contractions regular? Is she in a lot of pain?"

Another question to the side. Then, "Yes and yes." That definitely didn't sound like Braxton-Hicks.

While there was a staff doctor on duty in Labor and Delivery, my patient had suffered a great deal of emotional trauma this week. She was relying on my familiar presence. I had to be there and hope that the police would rescue Lenore.

"You're with her?" I asked.

"Yes. Duncan's here, too."

I was glad Tanya was among friends, especially Cress, who'd practiced to be Tanya's birthing partner. As for whether it would require a judge to determine who took little Georgie home, that had to wait.

"I'll meet you at the hospital," I said.

CHAPTER TWENTY-ONE

Someone must have sent a baby-gram alerting Safe Harbor's soon-to-be-born infants that they were missing a party, because Labor and Delivery had one of those nights when expectant moms filled every room and the surgical suites were booked nonstop.

I carried a go-bag in my trunk with a change of clothes in case I had to sleep in an on-call room, but there was no sleep for me Sunday night. Or in the early hours of Monday, either. If I hadn't arrived, the OB on duty would have been forced to summon backup.

Tanya's labor was progressing normally. Cress and Duncan took turns plying her with ice chips and encouragement. With her regular heartbeat, Baby Georgie seemed happily unaware of the tragedies and betrayals afflicting her family.

Since I was on hand, I delivered half a dozen other babies and performed two C-sections. Around four a.m., my other surrogate, Maggie, arrived with an entourage that included her husband and the intended parents.

Her membranes had ruptured, an occurrence better known as waters breaking. Although she wasn't having contractions, she was full term and had a placenta previa. We needed to proceed with the surgery.

"As long as the baby's okay, I'm fine with it," my patient told me. She seemed calmer than intended mother Danielle, whose hands were shaking.

"Then let's say happy birthday to this little lady," I remarked.

Less than an hour later, a seven-pound, five-ounce baby girl joined her overjoyed parents and the satisfied surrogate. In the hall, I ran into Danielle's sister, Celia, the nurse who'd donated the egg that had become her niece.

"I'm sorry Dr. Schwartz didn't arrive in time," she told me.

"She isn't his patient."

"He asked me to let him know when Maggie came in," Celia said.

"Why?" It seemed unlike the reserved Jeremiah.

"He feels a connection, I suppose because I'm his nurse." The red-haired woman favored me with a tilted smile. "I hated to wake him, so I texted. Guess he didn't hear it."

I refrained from commenting that my oddball colleague might sleep in a coffin with poor reception. That was unkind and, besides, he'd managed to respond to urgent summons during our residency. On one occasion, he'd arrived, grainy-eyed, when he hadn't been sent for. He'd dreamed that he got a call, he'd told me.

"After ten years as an OB, why is he suddenly taking an interest in babies?" If anyone understood Jeremiah, it would be Celia. Until she arrived the previous autumn, he'd driven away every nurse who assisted him. The two of them had clicked, professionally speaking.

"We all grow and change." She glanced at the wall clock. Nearly seven a.m. "You catching a few winks before office hours?"

"I'll hit the cafeteria instead." Hot food service should be available by now. "One of my patients is likely to deliver soon."

"The other surrogate." Her comment implied that she, like most of the staff, was aware of Tanya's situation. "Any more news on last night's murder?"

"Not that I've heard." In the crush of deliveries, I'd concentrated on the tasks before me. There'd been nothing I could do to help Lenore or anyone except my patients.

"Better eat while you can."

"See you later."

On my way, I got a text that Tory wanted to update me in person. I directed her to meet me in the cafeteria.

At the ground floor, the scent of frying bacon overwhelmed my healthier intentions. I piled my plate with bacon, eggs and a blueberry muffin.

Only a scattering of tables were occupied. I sat alone and had nearly finished breakfast when Tory arrived, tray in hand. Despite her businesslike appearance, crinkles around the eyes signaled that she, too, had had little if any sleep.

"Have they found Lenore?" I asked.

She took a sip of coffee. "Not yet. She hasn't contacted you?"

"No. Has Agatha's killer been identified?"

"Not that I'm aware of." My sister-in-law pushed a frizzy strand of hair behind her ear. "Soraya's in the clear. Keith was interviewing her when the murder went down."

"I'm surprised he shared that with you."

"He didn't. I talked to her directly." Between mouthfuls, Tory continued, "I asked how she got involved with Agatha. She said they ran into each other at the supermarket a few days ago and struck up a conversation."

Agatha had complained of her low pay, especially in light of her employers' wealth, and agreed to share a few confidences for cash. Once the reporter primed the pump, Agatha had gone after more tidbits, including an attempt to snoop on Morris.

"She went the extra mile," I said. "Literally."

"Yeah. If she weren't dead, I'd read her the riot act."

"She spilled the family secrets?" This I'd like to hear.

"Not entirely," Tory said. "Soraya believed Agatha was withholding the big stuff."

"Dangling for more money?"

A shrug. "Or fear of the consequences if she revealed too much."

Considering that Agatha's outburst at the gallery might have inspired her murder, it was a reasonable assumption. "Learn anything else?"

"Agatha owned a gun," Tory said. "It's missing. You didn't hear that from me." She must have received a tip from one of the buddies she retained from her years on the force, crime scene technicians and a few uniforms susceptible to the traditional doughnut bribery.

Why had Agatha had a gun? Had she been threatened?

"Scary to think who might have taken it." I piled flatware atop my empty plate.

"Don't leave yet. I'm saving the best for last." Tory drained her cup. "Be right back."

While she refilled her cup, I checked my cell. The charge nurse sent Tanya's latest stats, showing the baby was in no hurry, and I still had an hour and a half until office hours.

"What's this best you're saving?" I inquired as my sister-in-law parked her butt in her chair.

"Not sure I should share it till I've talked to Keith." She frowned at her phone. "He hasn't answered my text."

I reached out as if to grab her cup. "I'm holding this hostage until you talk."

"Okay, okay." She hung onto the cup for dear life. "I contacted Noah's old partner in San Francisco, Brad Assaf. I gather he's an uber-rich investor and tech blogger."

"You got hold of him in the middle of the night?"

"I posted on his blog site. He responded immediately and agreed to talk." She fixed me with a mock glare. "Quit interrupting."

"Yes, ma'am."

"According to Brad, Noah and Bianca were total party animals. After they sold the company and the Bryerlys retired to Safe Harbor, they flew down a bunch of friends to celebrate Parker's birth. Splashy party with celebrity entertainers, plus they rented hotel suites for everyone."

That didn't sound like my reclusive neighbors. "What changed?"

"Brad only knows it happened after they took a second honeymoon in Greece when Parker was a year old," Tory said. "They were planning another big get-together on their return. Also, he and Noah had been tossing around concepts for another start-up. After he got home, Noah denied any interest in a new venture, and cut off old ties."

"With everyone or just Brad?" The guy might be nursing a grudge.

"Everyone, according to him. He was flooded with inquiries about Noah's odd behavior. People assumed Brad would have the inside track, but he didn't."

Even the great-grandparents, who'd tended Parker during the Greece trip, had contacted Brad to ask what was up, Tory reported. Apparently, once Noah retrieved little Parker, he and Bianca had refused to allow visits until after Cress's birth more than a year later. Then Noah used to fly the kids to Texas once a year for a few days, without his wife.

Strange behavior. "Anything else?"

"Yeah," Tory said. "I asked if Noah had shared details of his childhood with Brad. About the fire that killed his parents or the period when he was in foster care."

"Did he?"

"Brace yourself."

I seized the edge of the table. "Earthquake?" They tend to start with a low rumble that I don't always register.

My sister-in-law laughed. "No, dumb-ass. I mean for the big revelation."

"Oh." In my defense, I hadn't slept all night. "Well?"

"Noah told Brad he'd had an identical twin brother named Norm," she said. "Norm died when they were eight. In case you have trouble counting, that was after their grandparents took them in."

What? Surely Lenore was aware of the twin, yet she hadn't mentioned him. "How did Norm die?"

"An accident," Tory said. "According to Brad, Noah wasn't sure what kind."

Another fire or drowning? There'd been an unusual number of out-of-hospital deaths in that family. And now the bizarre revelation about a twin.

Tory stretched her shoulders. "Interestingly, Brad claimed Bianca never smoked. Wouldn't let anyone smoke near her, either."

I felt as if I'd started assembling a jigsaw puzzle only to discover there were pieces that didn't fit the picture on the box. Unless it was the wrong picture entirely. But what was the right one?

"Did Brad talk to Noah face-to-face after Greece?" I asked.

"Nope."

"Not even once?"

"Negative."

That raised a possibility that sent a chill through my nervous system. "What if the twin didn't die?"

"That's what I'm wondering." She swallowed. "Can you imagine?"

"I'm trying." Two Bryerlys had flown to Greece for a holiday, and two Bryerlys had returned. What if it hadn't been the same couple?

An identical twin might pass for his brother, if he was clever and had done his research, especially considering the recent retirement and move across the state. And Bianca? With hair dye and cosmetics, a woman who resembled her could use her ID as long as she avoided people who knew the original.

Nine years ago, Saul and Lenore had moved to Safe Harbor. Once they met the woman passing as Bianca, surely they'd had suspicions.

Had Saul been vocal about that? Within a year, he'd fallen from a boat and drowned. *"They never identified the other guy, you know. The one Saul went fishing with."*

I'd attributed Lenore's remark to confusion. Maybe she'd been dropping a clue. Maybe she'd been dropping a lot of clues.

Or perhaps my tired brain was running wild after a hard night. "Tory, do you think they're fakes? If Noah and Bianca aren't really Parker's parents, they might not hesitate to frame him." I still hadn't figured out a reason for them to kill Wes, though.

"I'd rather not speculate." Tory arose stiffly. "Keith still isn't answering. I'd better find him. No matter how busy he is, he needs to hear this."

"I presume you don't feel obligated to tell your clients what you've learned."

"Nope. My contract is with Noah Bryerly." Tory lifted her tray. "And I'm beginning to doubt that's who signed it. Be careful, Eric."

"Me? You should warn Parker."

"He's not picking up his calls. Probably sleeping." She angled off between tables.

I stared across the cafeteria, stunned by these revelations.

What kind of snake's nest had Parker and Cress grown up in? If our speculation was correct, the Bryerlys were her parents, but not his. The man we knew as Noah would be Parker's uncle; Bianca was no relation at all.

Considering her long acquaintance with Bianca, Agatha must have suspected something was amiss. Learning that she'd been selling information to a reporter could have motivated these scoundrels to eliminate her.

Had they disposed of Lenore as well? Despite her dementia, she might sooner or later have spilled the truth. Unless I was jumping to ridiculous conclusions about the whole situation.

A ding from my phone drew me from my reverie. Must be an update about Tanya.

But the text was from Unknown Sender. It read: "Side park lot. Now. Trust no one. Please, Dennis."

Lenore! But she had no cell phone, according to Parker. This might be a trap.

I couldn't leave her out there alone. So I went.

CHAPTER TWENTY-TWO

The side exit opened onto a small parking lot reserved for department heads, the handicapped and short-term visitors to Labor and Delivery. I found it half-empty, and for a moment feared I'd misunderstood the message.

Along the far side, in shrubbery abutting my office building, something stirred. A metallic rod jutted from behind a large SUV, followed by a head of white hair flattened from its usual poofy cloud.

"Lenore?" I hurried across to her.

"There y'all are, sugar." With the aid of her walker, the elderly woman tottered into full view.

"I've been worried about you."

A bony hand gripped my wrist with surprising power. "Things are not what they seem, Eric."

She spoke with steely resolve. And used my correct name.

A quiver of anxiety ran through me. Agatha's gun was missing. Also, it didn't take much strength to strangle someone with a scarf. How well did I know this woman?

"I'd better call Keith." I took out my phone.

"Wait!" Her fingernails dug into my wrist. "Hear me out, Eric."

"Okay." I kept my tone calm. I'm not a big fan of getting shot, even by little old ladies. "Where have you been?"

"Hospital waiting rooms," Lenore said.

"All night?"

"When you're old, you're invisible."

I conceded the point. "How did you get here?"

"Uber. I'm not completely out of the loop," she said with a spark of her usual verve. "Aren't cell phones the best darn gadgets? Picked one up at the drugstore when Aggie wasn't watching. That poor woman! I saw on TV someone killed her."

"You weren't there?"

"No way was I sticking around after she flapped her mouth. I took off while she was on the potty." Releasing my wrist, Lenore steadied herself on the walker. "She was fake Bianca's cousin, did you know that? But I don't believe she had any idea what those two were capable of."

"Fake Bianca," I repeated. "Good name for her."

"Darn tootin'." Lenore's forehead furrowed. "Y'all aren't humoring me, are you, Eric? I won't have it! I'm trusting y'all to believe me."

If it weren't for Tory, I might not have. Dementia patients can become paranoid while trying to make sense of a world full of holes. There's a syndrome—Capgras delusion—in which the patient believes that a family member or friend has been replaced by an identical imposter. While most commonly associated with schizophrenia, this syndrome can occur with brain injury or dementia.

Today, Lenore didn't strike me as either confused or deluded.

"Is it true Noah had an identical twin named Norm?" I asked. "And that everything changed after that trip to Greece?"

Lenore's expression cleared. "Bless your heart. How did y'all find out? Oh, it must be your clever sister-in-law."

"It was," I confirmed. "While we're on the subject, who is fake Bianca, really?"

Lenore blinked against a shaft of sunlight. "Aggie used the name Cressida once or twice."

"Cressida, like her daughter?"

"Only Cress is nothing like her, thank the Lord. And thank the nanny who raised those two kids." At a burst of noise, Lenore flinched. It was only rap music from a car on the hospital's circular drive. "With her long hair and dark eyes, Cressida resembled the real Bianca, but her personality? Not sweet at all. Pure meanness."

"Long hair?" The Bianca I'd met wore it short.

"Cut it last spring."

"That was her in Wes's photograph?" It would explain a lot. Including Agatha's slaying after she dropped hints about the picture to me and to Keith, right in front of Noah.

"Yessiree," she said. "That slut was sleeping with her son-in-law. How do y'all like that?"

It repulsed me. Instead of replying, I asked, "All these years, did you know they were phonies?"

Lenore sighed. "For a long time, I wore blinders. The truth was too horrible to think about. Murdering those wonderful people, Parker's parents."

"And Saul?"

"He was mostly on the road when Noah—Norm—brought the kids to visit. Then he retired and we moved out here."

"He got suspicious?"

Her eyes watered. "After he spoke up about it, Norm killed him. That evil, evil man."

Yet she'd kept silent about it. "Why didn't you tell the police?"

"A twin back from the dead, passing for his rich brother? You suppose they'd believe a cockamamie story like that from an old fart like me?" Lenore retorted. "If they didn't lock me up, they'd have turned me over to my grandson. I'd have been stifled in my sleep."

I couldn't fault her logic. "Why not move back to Texas after Saul died?"

"I had to make sure Parker was safe. He'd noticed his dad was a darn ignoramus about computers and sooner or later he'd have asked too many questions. I didn't figure they'd do me in as long as I pretended to be nuts."

Chatter drifted to us around the corner of the office building. Staffers were arriving for work, and I needed to check on Tanya. But, for the moment, curiosity won out. "What happened to Norm when he was eight?" I'd gathered that both boys had been rescued from foster care. "Why did you tell his brother he'd died?"

She lowered her gaze. "We had to send him away. That boy set fire to my cat. He was laughing when Saul caught him. Poor little Whiskers had to be euthanized."

"He'd lost his parents and been in foster care," I said. "That could have messed him up, but with enough love..."

"Love couldn't save that child." Lenore's voice shook. "Noah was terrified of his brother. He said Norm set the fire that killed their parents."

Hard to believe. "Couldn't it have been an accident?"

"Norm set a lot of fires," Lenore answered. "Like I said, he thought it was funny. Saul reckoned we were all in danger. One day, he took Norm out and came home alone. He claimed he'd signed the boy over to some agency, and we told Noah he'd died in an accident."

"The boy didn't ask questions?" He'd been old enough to doubt the story.

"He was relieved, with good reason. There's something missing in Norm, the thing that makes us human. He covers it up well, though, now that he's older," Lenore said. "Fake Bianca's even worse. She spends most of her time at their properties in New York, Las Vegas and Rome. I have no idea what she does there and I'd rather not find out."

A comment of the caretaker's sprang to mind. "Agatha told Parker his family was cuckoo, or a word that sounded like it. Kah-KO. Any idea what that means in Greek?"

When Lenore hesitated, I thought she was about to plead ignorance. Then she said, "Yes, she mentioned it to me once and I asked her."

"And?"

"It means evil."

My hands went cold. Then my phone beeped with a text. It was good news. "Your great-great granddaughter's about to be born."

Lenore smiled. "Let's not keep her waiting."

We'd nearly reached the side entrance when a man opened it and blocked our path. Tight across his chest stretched a navy T-shirt reading "Ask Me About My Superpowers," while his "Geek" baseball cap hid all but a few wisps of white hair. If anyone spotted him, the description might point yet another finger at Parker.

Before I could react, Norm Bryerly grabbed the cell from my grasp. "Well, well. Here's Granny with her nosy friend."

"Get lost!" Lenore shouted.

"My phone," I ordered. "Now."

Norm ignored me. "Where the hell—oh, here she is."

Into the side lot sped a battered red Honda Accord. Parker's car, with fake Bianca at the wheel. She whipped it around and stomped to a halt alongside us.

We were caged in. With no way to pull Lenore to safety, I yelled, "Police! Somebody call 911!"

No response. Where was everybody?

"Shut up!" Norm swung hard. In a blinding flash, the edge of my cell phone caught me in the forehead. When my vision cleared, he was pointing a gun at me.

"Stop!" Lenore tottered toward him.

I braced for a shot.

"Not here, Noah, you idiot." Bianca grasped the old lady's arm. "Someone might spot us."

"Yeah, okay. Hand me the key."

Despite a curl of the lip, she obeyed, then forced Lenore into the front seat. At gunpoint, Norm shoved me into the back. If there was a smart move that could have saved the day, it eluded my throbbing brain.

Norm tapped a quick message into my cell before tossing it under a parked car. Taking the wheel, he passed the gun to his wife. "Keep this aimed at him. If he tries anything, shoot."

"Whatever." With a sneer, fake Bianca sat next to me. I must be interrupting her busy schedule of smoking, shopping and killing people.

The car sped forward. Through the window, I glimpsed patients and visitors flowing into the hospital's main entrance. How could Lenore and I be kidnapped right outside the hospital? Somebody had to notice.

No one did. When I tried to shout, my throat was too thick to move words.

"Where's Parker?" Lenore demanded. "What have you done with him?"

Norm kept his eyes trained ahead. "He got a text from you half an hour ago, Granny. Begging you to keep it secret that you're hiding in the wetlands. He should be out there searching—close to where they'll find your body."

"And this nosy doctor's," snarled fake Bianca.

"Nobody'll believe I ran off." My vocal cords had started working again, scratchily.

"I just answered the text on your phone," Norm announced as we swung onto Safe Harbor Boulevard. "How sweet. You're going rescue poor old Lenore in the wetlands."

"Y'all aren't fooling anyone," his grandmother snapped. "The police know your real names."

Norm's jaw twitched. "You're bluffing, you old fool."

"Norm and Cressida," I said.

"Damn it!"

I pressed on. "There's still time to let us out and head for Mexico."

"I'm not living the rest of my life broke and on the run," Bianca fumed. "Noah, take care of this."

"How? This is your bloody fault!" he roared. "You shouldn't have tricked me into killing Wes."

There was a confession, unforced and heard by two witnesses. Fat lot of good that would do us.

"What trick?" Her finger twitched on the gun. "He'd have bled us dry or turned us in."

"You're lying, you manipulative bitch." Norm hit the gas, hurtling us through a red light. "He had no idea why I attacked him. He kept apologizing for sleeping with you, as if I care."

"I swear!" Bianca insisted. "I confided in him and he threatened..."

"You'd never have been stupid enough or drunk enough to tell him the truth about who we are." Norm smacked the wheel. "You wanted revenge. That's what got us into this mess. Oh, shit."

He hit the brakes, stopping inches short of the bumper ahead of us. Traffic had halted to let a stray dog cross the road.

When Bianca swayed, I lunged for her wrist. With split-second timing, Norm twisted around. "No, you don't, you basta..." He broke off in a disbelieving, choking spurt of blood.

Lenore had flung herself at him. Something glinted in her

hand.

It was a scalpel.

CHAPTER TWENTY-THREE

"You killed my husband, but you won't kill me!" Lenore shrieked.

Norm flailed, attempting to block his attacker while clamping his hand over his neck to stem the blood loss. The car rolled forward, bumping a pickup truck.

In the rear seat, Bianca writhed and kicked as we fought for the gun. Both the cramped space and my medical training hampered me. My instincts shrank from breaking her delicate wrist bones and causing trauma to the nerves.

Then the barrel swung toward Lenore. Furious, I wrenched Bianca's arm, and the damn thing went off like a cannon.

My memory of the next moments is hazy: Bianca slumping, Lenore pausing with the scalpel in midair, a door yanking open and a man shouting something. I think it was "What the hell?", although my ears throbbed too hard from the gun blast to be sure. We must have been a nightmarish, blood-soaked sight.

After a blur of minutes, the police and an ambulance arrived. Norm was gasping for air. Bianca, her chest blasted at close range, didn't twitch.

While the police collected the weapons, paramedics put pressure on Norm's injury. From the blood's dark-red color, I presumed Lenore had hit the jugular vein. If she'd sliced the carotid artery, he'd have bled out in short order.

Lenore insisted the cops locate Parker. It took them a while to sort out what she meant. As for me, when I told the paramedics I had to deliver a baby, they thought I was delirious.

Declining treatment for my bruises, I called my nurse. Farrah informed me that Dr. Schwartz—Jeremiah—had delivered Tanya's baby. She promised to reschedule my morning patients and, at my request, to direct the police to my phone in the parking lot.

"Don't touch it yourself," I told her. "It's evidence." Thanks to Keith's complaints about witnesses interfering with crime scenes, I knew the police would want to photograph and examine the phone where it lay, assuming no one else had spotted it.

"Would you like me to pick up another one for you?"

I was glad she'd thought of that. A doctor has to be reachable. "You're an angel."

"I'm just glad you're alive," Farrah said.

"That makes two of us."

Keith showed up as did crime scene technicians, ambulances whisked the Bryerlys to Heights—which, unlike Safe Harbor, has an emergency room—and Parker was found unharmed. He'd followed the instructions in the bogus text, persuaded that it was from Lenore because it used a childhood nickname. Unable to remember where he'd left his car, and unaware that his "parents" had stolen it, he'd taken a cab to the wetlands.

My head still hurting, I peered into the back of Keith's car, where Lenore was sitting with the window open. "Thank goodness you brought the scalpel," I told her.

"I pinched it at the hospital," she said. "Do y'all think they'll arrest me?"

"Nobody's charging you with anything." I patted her purple-veined hand. "You saved my life."

She smiled. "And you saved mine."

An officer intervened. "Excuse me, doctor. You can sit in Detective Horner's car until they're ready to take your statement."

"Gladly." I accompanied him to the other vehicle.

An hour or so later, in an interview room at the police station, Keith listened grimly to my story. He'd already heard from Tory that morning and from Lenore, so my information about the Bryerlys' identities didn't surprise him.

"The press will run wild over this," he grumbled after we'd finished.

"How's Mr. Bryerly doing?" I asked, more from curiosity than concern.

"Still in surgery," he said. "Expected to survive."

"And his wife?" On second thought, I wasn't sure they'd actually been married.

"DOA." Dead on arrival.

By then, Tory had brought a change of clothing for me, since the police needed mine as evidence. They'd thoroughly photographed me and, with my permission, swabbed inside my cheek for DNA.

It was nearly noon. Although disgruntled that I refused to go home and rest, Tory drove me to my office. I checked in with Farrah and promised to return after lunch to handle the afternoon's appointments.

She fussed over my bruised forehead and urged me to watch for signs of a concussion. While I hadn't lost consciousness, I was aware that symptoms such as ringing in the ears, despite being attributable to the gunshot, could also indicate brain injury. Yet, whether due to denial or to doctor's ego, I refused to coddle myself.

On my way out, I ran into Jeremiah waiting for the elevator. He seemed different, despite the familiar dark, penetrating eyes, bony face and tall, thin build. Then I identified the change: an unaccustomed grin that humanized him.

"Thank you for taking care of my patient," I said. "You may have heard, I was waylaid."

"Eric, why did you not tell me what it was like?" he asked.

"What *what* was like?"

Jeremiah gestured as if impatient with the awkward flow of words. "Perhaps you have assumed that I, like you, have appreciated the miracle of birth. That was not accurate."

"Never?" I heard the elevator ding on the floor above ours.

"Not until now."

"Oh?" I was too shaken by the morning's events to speculate about what he meant.

"When I visited Celia's baby—her sister's baby—a panorama unfolded before me of a toddler, a child, a girl growing up," he said.

"You identified her with Celia?" That was understandable.

"Perhaps. But when I delivered the Bryerly baby, the same thing happened." He blinked. "Again, a whole world opened up."

"That's what I experienced the first time I delivered a baby in med school."

"Was that why you chose this specialty, and not because of your father?" Jeremiah asked.

"Yes."

"As always, you are a guidepost to me."

As always, he was an enigma to me, I mused.

At the hospital, we parted, him to the cafeteria and me to the patient rooms. Maggie was recovering without complications from her C-section, I was pleased to note when I examined her surgical wound. Beside the bed, Danielle blissfully cuddled her new daughter.

They must have heard of my ordeal—and noticed the large bruise on my forehead—but they didn't bring it up, to my relief. I had no desire to dwell on the morning's trauma. No doubt my psyche would clobber me in the days and nights to come, but for now, I preferred playing my normal role as the level-headed doctor.

After admiring the newborn, answering their questions and reviewing follow-up care, I moved to Tanya's room. Stepping inside, I discovered how utterly I'd been kidding myself.

The sense of grief and shock was overwhelming, from Cress's tear-stained face to Tanya's arms folded protectively across her chest. I'd never been squeamish at the bloody, smelly messes a doctor encounters, but this emotional wreckage nearly did me in.

Memories flooded my brain: Bianca Bryerly collapsing against the seat; Norm clamping his hand to his slashed throat; Lenore screaming.

"Eric!" Tanya said. "You're as pale as these sheets."

I drew up a chair. "My apologies."

"For what? Being human?" Only when Cress shifted position to touch my shoulder did I notice she was holding Georgie. "Don't worry. I won't drop her," she assured me. "She's all I have left."

"Except me," Tanya said.

Cress nodded. "Thank you, thank you, thank you. You went through such agony to give me my baby. Bless you."

Did this mean Tanya had dropped her idea of seeking custody? *Better phrase that carefully, Eric.* "Everything's resolved?"

"Thanks to Dr. Schwartz." Tanya played with a strand of blond hair that had escaped its clip.

How had Jeremiah, normally tone deaf to feelings, negotiated this minefield? "What did he say?"

In the bed, she dropped her hands to her lap. "He asked what I saw when I looked at Georgie. I said, an adorable baby. When he asked Cress the same question, she said, a future full of love, hard work and being there for her. That was when I understood that she's the real mother. I'm not ready for that level of—well, not sacrifice exactly."

"Commitment?" Cress suggested.

"Yeah, if I'm being honest." Tanya said. "It hurts to admit it. I love her, just not enough."

"That's very generous of you." I was glad to see this new maturity. Someday, Tanya would make a wonderful parent. At the right time.

Like me. No matter how much I yearned for a family, I had a lot of emotional undergrowth to clear away before I was ready. Too bad we can't hire a gardener to do the pruning and weeding for us. We have to get our hands dirty and scratched, branch by thorny branch.

"Dr. Schwartz was terrific." Tanya's voice drew me back to the hospital room. "But I wish you'd been here."

"We heard what happened." Cress struggled to swallow. "I can't take it in yet. That Mom's dead. That she and Wes..." Tears flowed down her cheeks. "Let's not talk about it. Take care of Tanya. Please."

"Of course." Steadied by concern, I rose to check the computer terminal and then my patient. There'd been no need for an episiotomy, the surgical cut once considered standard even in uncomplicated births. Save for soreness, Tanya was recovering well. "You're in great shape. You should be able to go home tomorrow."

"The pediatrician said Georgie can leave with me then, too," Cress put in.

A shadow of longing darkened Tanya's face. She banished it with a deep breath. "Duncan will pick me up. We're moving in together."

"He's been very supportive," Cress added. "You're lucky. After Wes, I'm not sure I'll ever trust a man again."

"You deserve to be loved," Tanya responded.

"How? I can't tell a liar from an honest person, since my parents lied to me all my life." When Georgie squirmed, Cress adjusted her position gently, and the baby curled against her.

"You'll be a great mom," I said.

"Will I?" The new mother lifted her head. "Detective Sparks told me what my parents did. My God! I was raised by monsters. My mother slept with my husband and then Dad murdered him. And they tried to frame my brother and kill you and Gran. If my parents are that evil, how can I be any better?"

"They're psychopaths, unable to empathize with other people's pain," I said. "That's not the case with you."

"You and Parker were raised by a nanny," Tanya reminded her. "You told me Dolores was like a second mother."

Or the only mother, in a sense. Bonding with a parent figure is essential for healthy child development, physically and mentally. How fortunate there'd been someone to step into the void.

"When I was ten, Dolores went to Honduras to raise her niece's children. I cried myself to sleep every night for weeks." Cress pressed on, urgently. "But aren't violence and selfishness in our DNA, Dr. Darcy?"

"There's an old dispute about which matters most, nature or nurture," I said. "The truth is, it's both. We may inherit tendencies such as poor impulse control or aggression, but heredity isn't the whole picture."

"It's a big part of it," she insisted.

"Your father and Parker's were identical twins, yet even as

children, they didn't behave the same, according to your great-grandmother."

She ducked her head. "Parker isn't really my brother, is he? I miss him so much. But after my parents murdered his parents, he must hate me. No wonder he hasn't called."

"The police are probably still interviewing him," I said. "I doubt he blames you for any of this."

Cress sniffled. "As far as I'm concerned, he's my brother and always will be."

"Of course he is," Tanya said stoutly.

I was weary, hungry and keenly aware that I'd promised to treat patients that afternoon. "Take time to heal, both of you," I said. "Watch for feelings of despair, irritability, flashbacks and difficulty sleeping that can indicate depression. Cress, don't isolate yourself with Georgie. And please get counseling if problems persist."

"Okay." Hardly an enthusiastic response. Then a smile flickered. "Don't worry, doc. I'll be careful."

After a quick lunch, I honored my commitment to my afternoon patients. Plunging into work felt good, allaying or at least postponing further stress reactions.

Over the next few days, my physical injuries healed, while my emotions remained chaotic. There were nightmares, along with vivid flashbacks. I startled easily, and kept scanning my surroundings for danger. An undercurrent of anxiety persisted, as if I'd been awakened to the presence of an earthquake fault directly beneath my feet. Only when I concentrated on patients did the symptoms disappear.

As Tanya recovered, she told me she missed the baby she'd carried for nine months. She and Duncan were discussing having a baby together, once they'd saved enough money. "It was a great experience, in spite of everything."

"Don't rush," I cautioned. "You've been through a lot. Your

body needs to recover."

"I promise," Tanya said jauntily. "And I know I wasn't Georgie's real mother. But with a supportive dad who loves me, it'll be a different story."

Her optimism buoyed my spirits, yet within hours, the darkness returned. To avoid inflicting my moods on others, I mostly stayed home, ate little and buried myself in reading.

As details emerged about the Bryerly case, I followed them avidly. Norm spoke freely to the police and, ignoring his attorney's advice, insisted on pleading guilty to his son-in-law's murder without a prosecution deal. He seemed relieved to heave a lifetime of lies off his chest.

The narrative went like this: After growing up in foster homes, he'd passed his twenties as a petty criminal, primarily committing identity theft. To escape prosecution, he'd fled to Europe, where he'd traveled from country to country, playing guitar and singing while charming money from gullible women.

In Athens, he'd had an affair with Cressida Floros, a petty criminal working as an unlicensed tour guide. She'd steered him to a job with a scammer friend, selling counterfeit merchandise and overbilling tourists' credit cards.

One fateful day, she'd taken an astonished glance at two wealthy Americans and recognized a golden opportunity. The man, tech entrepreneur Noah Bryerly, was identical to her boyfriend, while his wife bore a passing resemblance to Cressida. She'd quickly learned their schedule and where they were staying.

Initially, she'd intended to exploit their credit and raid their bank accounts, until she described the couple to Norm and he realized this must be his twin. Based on their research and what he knew about his brother, they'd begun orchestrating a much bigger crime.

The couple had invited the Bryerlys to dinner, where Noah

was puzzled but overjoyed to discover that his brother had survived. Norm explained that their disciplinarian grandfather, intolerant of childish antics, had sent the boy away and lied about it. A persuasive tale, considering that it was based on truth and that Noah had long forgotten his childhood fears of his twin.

Happy to be reunited with family, Noah and Bianca had spilled details of their lives. Norm and Cressida had soaked it up, especially the fact that the pair had recently moved away from friends and colleagues. By morning, they'd put the finishing touches on their brutal plan.

That day, two couples went sailing. Only one couple returned.

Norm admitted to having garroted his brother, while Cressida had stabbed Bianca. They'd emptied their victims' pockets and thrown the bodies into the sea.

"Killing my brother—it's haunted me for thirty years," Norm was reported as saying. "But I figured he'd had an easy life and it was my turn."

Cressida had dyed her hair the same shade as Bianca's. On their return, they claimed to have fallen ill with high fevers while in Greece, to explain lapses in memory. Norm timed his visits to Texas to coincide with Saul's absences on the road, while Lenore soon discovered that asking questions led to fewer visits with the grandchildren.

For decades, they'd passed as their victims. After Cressida bore her namesake daughter, they'd hired a nanny, and Parker grew up believing these were his parents. The Bryerlys had avoided making close friends in California, spending several months each year at their other homes and often traveling separately.

No one had asked awkward questions until nine years ago, when Lenore and Saul, who'd retired from driving a truck, moved to Safe Harbor. As the months passed, Saul's suspicions intensified.

Norm had suggested they go fishing together to clear the air. Away from shore, he beat Saul to death, disguising the injuries to appear accidental.

However, Norm had resisted Cressida's demand that he kill Lenore. She was no threat because of her dementia, he'd pointed out, and another death might raise questions. He admitted to having a fondness for his grandmother, while he'd loathed his grandfather for abandoning him to foster care.

Some fondness, I thought. It hadn't stopped him from scheming to kill her when she became inconvenient.

They'd hired Cressida's cousin, Agatha, an impoverished widow, to watch over the old lady. She'd been the only person they trusted who knew their true identities.

There'd been no great affection between the Bryerlys, who'd agreed they were free to conduct affairs away from Safe Harbor. Noah hadn't much cared what his wife did until she foolishly fell for Wes, proud that she was still beautiful and sexy enough to steal a handsome young man from her own daughter.

When Wes threw her over for Tanya, the fake Bianca had become obsessed with revenge. This, combined with her vicious nature, led to their downfall.

She'd told her husband that, while drunk, she'd revealed the truth about their identities to Wes and that he'd threatened to reveal all if they didn't fork over a million dollars. Although furious at her stupidity in disclosing their secret, Norm had initially believed her, since he already despised Wes. In his way, he loved his daughter, and he knew Wes was cheating on her.

It wasn't clear whether it was Norm or Cressida who hit on the idea of framing Parker. Either way, it served their interests by diverting the police and removing a potential danger. Norm might have served as a passable father figure over the years, but by openly questioning why the former programming genius had such a sketchy understanding of coding, his "son" had, in his view, become a threat.

Because of his inability to empathize, this heartless man had badly miscalculated. Worried about the possibility of dementia, Parker had been eager to help his father, not to unmask him.

The night of the dinner party, Norm had used Parker's phone to lure Wes to the harbor. To allay suspicion the next morning, he'd told Wes that he'd accidentally texted with the wrong phone. Norm had said he merely wanted to clear the air.

The same pretext he'd used with Saul, eight years earlier. Not original, but effective.

He'd brought Lenore's cane, claiming he had a stiff leg, and suggested they go for a walk. Norm had handed his son-in-law a drugged bottle of flavored water from a company in which Norm had invested, requesting an unbiased opinion.

Once they reached the wetlands, the older man had attacked. Despite the drug, Wes fought back. The murder had been a violent business that involved clubbing the victim and stabbing him with Parker's knife. Afterward, Norm had disposed of his bloody clothing and worn long sleeves to cover his bruised arms.

As for Agatha's murder, he blamed that entirely on Cressida. She'd excused herself from dining with a group of local dignitaries, citing the time difference for having to place an overseas business call relating to a clothing line she claimed to be designing. Norm had gone to "check" on her a couple of times, maintaining the cover that she was on the restaurant premises while becoming increasingly aware that she must have gone to confront the caretaker.

As I'd surmised, they'd believed that Agatha had turned against them. Although she hadn't been prepared to spill the whole tale, she'd dropped heavy hints at the gallery about the naked picture of Bianca.

Much of Norm's confession couldn't be confirmed, and it was unclear whether the district attorney's office or any other authority would file charges in Saul's death, Agatha's murder or the slayings in Greece. For killing Wes, Norm faced a minimum of life in prison. That left four murder victims who might never receive justice.

In an article, Soraya commented that while Westlake Choate had chosen secrets and shadows as his artistic turf, he'd been tragically unaware of the secrets and shadows in his wife's family. The shocking revelations benefited the Wine Arts Gallery, where crowds swarmed to view Wes's photos. The entire collection sold, despite further boosts in price.

I couldn't imagine how these revelations were affecting Parker, who'd secluded himself in the family home with Cress, her baby and their great-grandmother. He'd cut himself off from friends, including Barry. The police might solve a crime, but they can't undo the damage.

On Saturday, less than a week after being kidnapped, I resumed jogging. It felt good to breathe the sea air as I followed the route to Pelican Lane. Beyond Keely's house, the wetlands lay quiet, undisturbed by carrion birds or, presumably, dead bodies.

On my way home, I was pleased to hear the creak of a walker and spot Lenore Bryerly halting at the intersection of our streets, her smile bright beneath her white hair. A bruise on her arm was the only visible sign of her ordeal.

Her companion, a middle-aged woman with gray-brown hair and a pleasant face, waited beside her. Unlike the late Agatha, she showed no impatience to shepherd her charge home.

"Eric," Lenore greeted me. "This is Anna, my new helper."

We exchanged handshakes and greetings. Then I asked Lenore how she was doing.

"The police are holding onto my favorite cane. I'll be glad when the new one I ordered gets here," she said. "This walker makes me look like an old lady."

I chuckled. "I'm glad you aren't really suffering from dementia."

Lenore shrugged. "Some old folks long to be young again. I'm just tickled pink I can act like myself."

"She's sharp as a tack," Anna put in. "Her great-grandson's teaching her to use a computer."

"Got a lot of Facebook friends," Lenore added. "They say I'm an inspiration to them. But that's not why I called you here today, Eric."

"Oh, did you?"

She leaned on her walker. "It's Parker. His whole world's upside down and he's lost. Can't think straight, hardly talks and won't eat. He just sits around and sulks."

I was sorry to hear that. "I've been concerned about him."

"I know he's not your patient," Lenore said. "But I want y'all to march up there right now and give him a talking-to."

I didn't bother to argue. "Will you join me?"

She waved her hand. "Oh, he won't listen to his great-grandma. Besides, Anna and I are going to play laser tag."

Her helper laughed. "No, we aren't."

"Eat one of those maple pecan things at the Waffle House, then."

Anna nodded. "That's doable."

Most likely Parker would dismiss me as an unwelcome busybody, but if I didn't try, I'd be hearing from Lenore. And let's face it, I was curious to see him. "I'll do my best."

"I knew I could count on you, hon."

I accompanied them up the block to Anna's car, then continued alone to talk to Parker. Or get the door slammed in my face.

CHAPTER TWENTY-FOUR

As I approached the glassed-in house, the angle of the light allowed a glimpse into the gold-and-white interior. Was it my imagination or had the place become less opaque?

I pressed the bell. Instead of a passage from *La Bohème*, the chimes played the theme from *Star Wars*.

The man who opened the etched-glass door had familiar heavy brows and broad cheekbones, but his eyes were sunken. In the space of two weeks, Parker Bryerly had left behind his geekish innocence.

"Eric," he said. "What brings you here?"

Might as well be frank. "Lenore sent me."

"A royal command." He stepped aside. "Can't fight that."

In the living room, I noted a baby blanket tossed over a chair and a stroller tucked behind the couch. "Is Cress home?"

"She's sleeping. Should I fetch her?"

"No. I'm here to see you."

"Figures."

Not exactly welcoming. In fairness, I'd arrived uninvited. Still, I felt as if I had a mission beyond what Lenore had charged me with.

Sometimes I land in a place or situation with no idea what

I'm doing there except for the nagging sense that there's a purpose. Whether it's for myself or for the other person, or both, isn't always apparent. This was one of those occasions.

Parker selected an armchair. In contrast to his former sprawl, he held himself upright, long legs stretched in front. His solid-blue T-shirt stuck to his rib cage.

I restrained the impulse to advise him about the importance of nutrition. He was a neighbor, not a patient.

"Do you plan to stay here?" I asked. "The house must have painful associations."

"My parents bought it." Parker wiggled his toes. Mature or not, he still didn't wear shoes at home. "My real parents. The ones who loved me."

I didn't bother with platitudes. After my wife's death, I'd developed a distaste for people who claimed that God never sends a burden greater than we can bear. Did that mean if I'd been weaker, Lydia would have survived?

Instead, I indulged my curiosity. "Has your uncle contacted you?"

"He requested I visit him in the hospital." Parker's fingers dug into the padded chair arms.

Fascination dragged me deeper into none-of-my business territory. "Did you?"

"Yeah. I'm not sure why. To see how he looks now that I know the truth, I guess," he said.

I pushed on. "And?"

"He's this total fake." Parker's voice rang with tension. "His eyes are too small and his wrinkles are in the wrong places. Maybe it's just me, but I think it's because he quit pretending to be something he isn't, like a decent human being."

He'd get no argument from me. "What did he say?"

"He apologized. Big deal! And said he hadn't done too bad a job of raising me, had he?" Parker scowled. "If there hadn't been a cop present, I'd have punched him."

"I wouldn't blame you," I said, although, in view of Norm's greater bulk and experience at beating people to death, I was glad his nephew hadn't had to fight him. "Did he say anything else?"

"Yeah." A trace of satisfaction eased the young man's grimness. "Can you believe, he offered me half his property? All puffed up, proud of his generosity. I informed him that it's my property, all of it. Not a penny for his defense, if he decides to mount one. Not a cent for anything."

"How'd he take it?"

"It shut him up, for once."

Parker explained that he'd consulted the estate attorney whose name I'd given to his sister. The lawyer had recommended that, based on Norm's confession and the parents' absence for more than thirty years, he seek a court order directing that death certificates be issued for them.

"They wrote a will before their trip," he said. "Gran still has it with a bunch of legal papers. They left me the house and their entire fortune."

After decades of high living, how much remained? "Isn't most of it gone?"

Parker's mouth twisted. "Surprisingly, Norm was pretty good at money management. Most of his business investments paid off and the properties he bought have appreciated a bunch. I can live well, establish a charity and fund a start-up I've been considering. Of course, I'll take care of Gran and Cress and the baby, too."

"That's kind of you." I was pleased he harbored no ill will toward his sister or, rather, cousin.

"And Tanya deserves a financial reward for acting as the surrogate, especially considering how Wes messed with her," Parker said.

"I'm sure she'll appreciate it."

"Duncan's a straight-up guy. I'm glad they're together." He sounded almost like his old, blithe self.

"You're handling this well," I ventured.

"Not really." His hands formed fists against his thighs. "The press is speculating that Dad... my uncle might duck the death penalty because he confessed. It makes me so mad I can't sleep. I'm glad Gran stabbed him and you shot that evil woman. I hope it hurt them like they hurt my mom and dad."

"I understand." While it had bothered me to have fired the shot that killed Bianca, I'd done it in self-defense. Despite lingering bad feelings, I refused to accept any guilt. "How's Cress taking all this?"

I hadn't talked to her since that day at the hospital. Although I presumed Cress would continue as my regular patient, only the surrogate was seeing me for postnatal care. Baby Georgie's checkups involved a pediatrician rather than me.

The revelations and deaths must be raw. She'd lost almost everyone, along with her faith in her husband and her parents.

"She's mad, too," he said. "What her mom did was unspeakable, and her father's just as bad. He should rot in prison."

His pain resonated with me, like a shrill tone that vibrates into your teeth. "Your anger is justified. Still, hanging onto it could be unhealthy."

He rose and paced furiously. "Prison is better than he deserves. I missed my whole childhood with my parents. I want those thirty years back!"

"I know how you feel." And wished I didn't. But there it was, that rage rising inside me again.

"Do you?" Parker planted himself in front of me. "Don't patronize me, Eric."

"The hell I am." Words erupted in a torrent. "I'd do almost anything to have Lydia here, just for a few minutes. To ask why she left. Whether she ever loved me. If I had answers, maybe I could forgive her."

He registered my point with a nod. Then resumed pacing.

"I'll never forgive those vipers," Parker said. "I have nightmares about my parents dying, believing they'll be forgotten, terrified of how those monsters will treat their son. How do you talk to the dead? How do you let go of *their* suffering?"

"I wish I knew. I haven't visited Lydia's grave in Israel because..." *Because why, Eric?* "Because if I do and there are no answers, I'll have to accept that there never will be, and I'm not ready for that."

"Me, either," he said. "Only my folks don't have graves."

Deep in the house, a baby wailed. Georgie was awake and Cress must be, too. Rising, I shook hands with Parker. "Sorry to intrude."

"No problem," he said.

I left doubting I'd done any good, for Parker or myself. That night, though, instead of hibernating, I joined my sister-in-law and Morris for dinner. When Barry dropped by, he and Tory and I went to the cop bar, where we ran into Keith and played several rounds of darts.

I don't remember who won except that it wasn't me. Nor did I care. I was happy to be away from grim thoughts that had worn out their welcome.

Trauma doesn't release its grip in a day. There would be dark moments ahead, but for whatever reason, I'd turned a corner.

A few weeks later, Parker flew to Greece, he told me afterwards. He hired a guide to show him around the area nicknamed the Athenian Riviera, where Norm had admitted murdering Noah and Bianca on a rented sailboat.

From there, he'd visited Cape Sounion, site of the Temple of Poseidon, where the guide mentioned that, during the Middle Ages, pirates had hidden in the nearby bay to prey on passing ships. According to legend, the area was haunted by the restless spirits of their victims.

A sense overwhelmed Parker that, for decades, his parents had been among the ghosts wandering the region's dry hills and curving coastline. He'd arranged for the guide to leave him at a waterfront *taverna* near where his parents must have died.

Staring out at the intensely blue Aegean Sea, Parker had sat alone and talked to the real Noah and Bianca. Maybe he addressed them in his mind, or let the people around him assume he was speaking into a headset, or just didn't care what anyone thought.

He assured his parents he was fine, that he knew the truth and that the murderers were paying for their crimes. He explained that he had a cousin who was like a sister, and how Lenore had survived by her wits. He described his plans, which their money would help to accomplish.

By the end of the day, he told me, he felt their spirits soar, free to let go and find peace at last. Then Parker came home and began his life anew.

And I went on with mine, grateful to be with people I loved and patients I cared about, no matter what unexpected paths they might lead me on.

The End

ABOUT THE AUTHOR

A former Associated Press reporter and TV columnist, *USA Today* bestselling author Jacqueline Diamond has sold more than one hundred novels. These include mysteries, medical romances, Regency romances and romantic comedies published by Harlequin, St. Martin's Press, William Morrow and Five Star Mysteries, among others. Jackie and her husband live in Southern California.

Jackie is best known for her Safe Harbor Medical romances and mysteries. Among the titles are *The Case of the Questionable Quadruplet*, *The Case of the Surly Surrogate*, *The Case of the Desperate Doctor* and *The Case of the Long-Lost Lover*.

You can sign up for her free newsletter and learn more about her books at her website, www.jacquelinediamond.net.

If you enjoyed this novel and are willing to post a short review at your favorite online book sites, it would be much appreciated. Thank you!

www.ingramcontent.com/pod-product-compliance
Lightning Source LLC
Chambersburg PA
CBHW020110180626
46812CB00006B/2552